When things get toug
And make you screa
When bills need pay
And you haven't a b
When things really s
Much worse than you
Take heart from the folks
Down Casey's Court

(They've all been through it!)

J.F.

28/12/90

With love to Alec,
Jackie & family.

Jo

By the same author

Casey's Court

JO FOX

Casey's Court Forever

GRAFTON BOOKS
A Division of the Collins Publishing Group

LONDON GLASGOW
TORONTO SYDNEY AUCKLAND

Grafton Books
A Division of the Collins Publishing Group
8 Grafton Street, London W1X 3LA

A Grafton Paperback Original 1990

ISBN 0-586-20562-4

Printed and bound in Great Britain by
Collins, Glasgow

Set in Times

'Get back to Rosamund Street where you belong!' shouted the woman from the tripe shop, shattering my hopes for a peaceful New Year.

The whole street was out today! Up and down the row of grimy terraced houses, the excited cries rang out as brazen Peggy Wells bravely squared up to fat Lucy from No. 1. 'I'll teach yer to steal my old man, Peggy bloody Wells!' she cried, rolling up her sleeves, and taking out her precious false teeth (which, to my disgust, she promptly slapped into my hand). 'Keep hold o' these, Jessy,' she said. 'I'd rather break me neck than me best teeth.'

'Steal him!' yelled Peggy Wells with a sneer. 'The bugger ain't *worth* stealing. I let 'im 'ave 'is wicked way because I felt sorry for the poor old sod. And looking at *you*, I can understand *why* 'e were bloody desperate!'

That did it. There was no holding fat Lucy now. In a minute, she'd surged forward to launch herself at the brazen hussy, and in another minute, they were locked in mortal combat, encouragement coming from all sides.

'Go on, Lucy . . . you teach the bugger a lesson!' yelled Sonya, arms folded across her bulbous cleavage.

'Send 'er back where she came from, the randy cow. There ain't no room round 'ere for the likes o' that one!' cried my Maggie.

I nearly fell over when Bertha Twistle loudly added her protest. 'None of us husbands is safe from her sort,' she shouted, 'not even my old Fred.' A bit different from what she told me in a huff some three weeks back, when she complained that he was 'shrivelled up at both ends, and neither use nor ornament to anybody'.

5

Some ten minutes later, following a lot of scuffling, yelling and rolling about, Peggy Wells was sent on her way, black eye and all. 'That's shown her, ain't it?' declared the jubilant Lucy, who was staggering around with the shirt hanging off her back, one of her stockings wrinkled round her ankle, and the sorry beginnings of *two* black eyes beneath her tousled brown hair. 'The bugger won't show her face round here again in a hurry. Now she knows what the women o' Casey's Court are made of!' While we were giving a cheer, she fell to the ground in a dead faint.

Long after Peggy Wells left for pastures new, though, her parting words still echoed over the cobbles. 'If yer think it's just fat Lucy's man I've had my fun with, you can think again! I've had *every* man down Casey's Court . . . 'cause none of you can satisfy the poor buggers!' (Talk about putting the cat among the pigeons!)

It's been a long hard day, and I for one am ready for my beauty sleep. It's a good job Wilhelmina didn't tell anybody else what she'd seen when running after Peggy Wells, to make sure she hadn't kidnapped our Tom. 'Ooh, Mam!' she said, all wide-eyed and wondering. 'You should have seen all the men waiting round the corner, queuing up for a kiss from Peggy Wells . . . and Fred Twistle was the first!'

I stopped her right there. 'Don't you tell another soul what you saw,' I told her (feeling secretly relieved when she smugly added, 'Barny Singleton wasn't there, though'). I pretended not to care whether he was there or not. He upset me twice last week, and I'm not about to forget in a hurry. If I'm honest with myself, I just can't see the two of us ever getting married. Half the time we're at loggerheads, and the other half I'm too besotted with him to see his faults (which both Maggie and Sonya are always pointing out to me).

Well, good night, Lord. Isn't it strange how things turn out? I feel as though I've lived in Casey's Court all my life, when in fact it's been only eighteen months since that clapped-out car coughed and spluttered its way northwards towards this little corner of Lancashire that's become home to all the family. I never thought I'd say it, but I really love Casey's Court and all the grand, wonderful, nosy, aggravating, crude, eccentric and delightful folk who live in its tiny crumbling terraced houses. (May the Council see fit to let them stand forever!)

My old mother, bless her heart, used to say, 'When one door closes, another opens,' and she was right. Whoever would have thought it, though? When that no-good womanizing husband of mine kicked the bucket, leaving me up to my neck in debt and homeless, this little northern legacy was the only hope I had. And here I am, many adventures later, with the hairdresser's business flourishing, and a weakness for 'meat and tattie pies'. I never would have believed that a born and bred southerner like myself could be so happy in a small Coronation Street-type community, so far behind the march of progress that the older women here still wear pinnies and turbans, and whitestone their front steps.

It's been an uphill struggle but, in all, it's been worth it. Thank you, Lord. Oh, and while I think of it, could you keep an eye on Sonya? I've tried to persuade her into giving up the shady part of her life and all those kinky men who queue up at her door, but she'll have none of it. 'The poor sods are lonely misfits in society,' she argues. When I pointed out that when all was said and done they were nothing but perverts, she promptly agreed, saying she'd bear that in mind. Some time later she told me I was quite right, and because of their peculiarities she was the only one they could turn to. Therefore, she had come to a decision which should meet with my approval.

'Oh, Sonya, that's wonderful!' I said, feeling as though at long last I had got through to her – then gobsmacked when she cried triumphantly, 'I've put me prices up, an' they're all paying an extra quid each!' So you see, Lord, it's up to you now. I do worry about her, because she's the best friend I've ever had, and in spite of her dubious pastime she has a heart of gold. Do your best for her, won't you? And try not to be too harsh on her, Lord. Treat her as one of your fallen angels.

Thursday, January 5th

It seems as though the Council has altogether given up trying to demolish Casey's Court, because it's been eighteen months since we had to put up the barricades in the street. There have been several meetings and countless letters going to and fro, but I think we're bringing them round to our point of view: that Casey's Court is an important part of old Lancashire's history, and as such should be preserved. I'm proud of my Maggie, bless her . . . I can't think of anybody I would rather have for a mother-in-law than her. What other woman of her advancing years would stand on an upturned orange box every Saturday in the middle of the market-place, singing the praises of Casey's Court, airing her views and washing her dirty linen for one and all? 'I've been a sinner,' she tells them unashamedly, her big frame shaking with emotion and tears welling up in her piggy blue eyes, 'but the folk of Casey's Court took me to their hearts and forgave me.' (Goodness! Her crime wasn't murder, for heaven's sake . . . just knicker-pinching!) 'Casey's Court folk are a breed on their own . . . a small caring community of people who help and love each other. Do we really want to let such a warm and wonderful neighbourhood die? There's only one name for the thugs from the Council who want to demolish Casey's Court – vandals! We must defend ourselves! Show the blighters that we mean business! Come on, rally round, folk. Send the Council packing!' So excited is she by this time that when Maggie climbs down from her orange box and heads towards the town hall half the population of Oswaldtwistle goes with her . . . all decrying those 'faceless monsters' who would heartlessly rip apart such a splendid place as Casey's Court.

While Maggie's inciting the crowd to violence, our Ethelbert stands close by, proudly waving his stick and gazing up at his famous wife with adoring eyes. 'My Maggie shoulda been Prime Minister,' he says, choking back the tears. It is a shame, bless the poor old fool, because when they all march out of the market with big Maggie up front holding the banner, emblazoned with the words 'Casey's Court Forever', it always seems to be him that cops the fruit and veg which comes sailing through the air to shouts of 'Gerrout of it, yer silly buggers' and 'You want locking up, the lot of you'. More often than not, such jeering and a few well-aimed gherkins stimulate one or two choice retaliations from the departing militants, such as 'Arse'oles!' and 'Come 'ere an' say that, yer bloody pissant!' Whereupon can be heard the piercing shrieks of Red Indians in full charge before the whole place is in a state of pandemonium, with arms, legs and a prime assortment of greengrocery flying about in all directions. I only went once and was in fear for my life. And though it's not so cheap and fresh, I find it safer to get my fruit and veg from the woman at the tripe shop. But I have written to the Queen about the whole sorry state of affairs. (No doubt she'll have something to say about it.)

Do you know, I was *amazed* when the woman from the tripe shop told me the Council had been inundated with applications from folk wanting to move into Casey's Court. 'It's your old Maggie,' she said proudly, 'she's making us famous.' That may well be, but I've got a horrible feeling she may also be putting the Council's back up – not to mention possibly attracting the wrong kind into our little neighbourhood. After all, who wants cabbage-pelting vandals living next door, eh? And I don't think I could stand another half-dozen banner-marching Maggies!

Dear Lord, save us from invasion.

Friday, January 6th

My corns are back with a vengeance. I've never known the shop so busy; what with numerous beard-trims, two bleaches, half a dozen Mohican cuts and three manicures, Sonya and I have been run off our feet. I was a fool to accept Maggie's offer of help . . . she gets so excited. I certainly had some fast explaining to do when she gave Betty Butler a short back and sides, with a full shave thrown in. The poor dear went into one of her fits – thrashing her arms about in such a frenzy that both Smelly Kelly and little Larkin up and fled. Poor little Larkin's retreating back end let off a volley of such frightening proportions that old Fred Twistle thought his water pipes had erupted, and promptly sent for the Council!

Then, as if that wasn't enough to be going on with,

Sonya's blouse got ripped open. When this ginormous pink bouncing chest burst out, the man from the takeaway swallowed his false teeth and we had to call an ambulance. (I don't think I can take much more. My nerves are going!)

Saturday, January 7th

Another busy day! Much as I had been looking forward to an evening out with Barny, I had to call it off. I felt so worn out when the shop closed that I couldn't be bothered to get myself ready. 'You'll be sorry, my girl!' warned Maggie, with a wag of her finger. 'When your teeth fall out and your hair turns grey . . . and you've gone to fat. You'll wish you'd made the best of your looks then, I can tell you!'

That made me feel miserable. I felt worse when Wilhelmina piped up, 'And anyway you've already got squiggly wrinkles all round your eyes!'

Of course, little Tom had to put in his two-penn'orth. 'When I hug you, Mammy, I can't get my arms right round you any more!' (I must be going to pot!)

Though when I looked in the mirror just now I was pleasantly surprised. All right, so I'm not as reed-slim as I was, and I do look tired. But my hair is still that pretty golden colour, and I do have nice firm breasts, with a shapely pair of pins. 'Isn't it a shame when people grow old,' piped up Wilhelmina from the bed-covers, 'and you used to be so pretty, Mam.' (I never have liked bloody kids!)

What with one thing and another, I've got a lot on my mind at the minute. Not the least of which is Barny Singleton. I'm convinced he's quietly fuming about my

11

rival hairdressing business beginning to do so well. I know I'm taking his custom. Sometimes I wonder if he's only keeping company with me so he can keep tabs on what I'm doing and pounce at the first opportunity to close me down. As Maggie and Sonya keep warning me, 'Stay on your guard, Jessy. Beneath that handsome exterior lurks a ruthless snake-in-the-grass!' I tell them they're wrong, but deep down I have a sneaky feeling they might just be right. But I do love him.

There's something else, as well. The other night, when Wilhelmina and Tom were coming back from the chip shop, they *both* claimed to have seen a woman in Barny's front parlour. I made little of their chatter and chastised them for looking into other people's windows. But I couldn't get it out of my mind. 'Real pretty, she was, Mam,' said little Tom, his big dark eyes swivelling in his head as he rammed a hot chip in his mouth, 'with long black hair all the way down to her belly!'

Wilhelmina's description stabbed a little closer to the heart. 'Just like a film star, she was.' It was plain to me that the little monsters were enjoying themselves – they never did like me and Barny courting. 'Honest, Mam . . . she did have long wavy black hair, and long eyelashes an' all. Oh, and you should have seen how tiny her skirt was!' At least the little madam had the decency to be shocked.

Having already worked myself up into a state, I ruthlessly packed them both off to bed when little Tom blurted out, 'And she has bigger tits than Sonya!' Really, Lord, can't you have more control over your children?

When I casually mentioned it to Barny later, he looked quite taken aback at first. Then he laughed, gave me a hug and told me that the kids were seeing things. If that was the case, why did he go so quiet afterwards? Oh, I do hope he's not two-timing me. That would be the last straw! I tell you one thing, though – if I ever catch him at it his feet won't touch the ground! Nor hers neither. As Sonya put it, 'Her long black hair will come in handy for swinging the bugger over the chimney tops, gal!'

Sunday, January 8th

I hate Sundays! The mornings aren't so bad, because it's all work right up to one o'clock. It's when everybody's laid out afterwards, stuffed full of meat and Yorkshire pud, that gets on my nerves. There's Maggie and Ethelbert tangled up together on the sofa, fast asleep and holding loud raspberry conversations with their naked gums; and both sets of false teeth eyeing each other in the fruit bowl. The kids usually start out stretched over the carpet, facing the telly with their chins on their hands. They always end up fighting and arguing, until I threaten to send them upstairs. Then, after a bit of sulking, they either clear off out or they fall asleep from boredom.

It's at times like these that I wish I'd learned to darn. I could start with the two black snoring holes gaping at me from the sofa.

I usually stand it for an hour or so before I rush to Sonya's for refuge – never forgetting her instructions: 'Never burst in, gal, 'cause ye'll frighten me punters off. Allus put yer ear to the door first. An' if there ain't no squeals o' delight nor screams o' terror comin' from upstairs, well then, give the door a good knocking, gal, an' I'll be there in no time at all!'

Though I think the world of Maggie, I can never understand why she insisted on her and Ethelbert's coming to live at *our* house when they got married. After all, Sonya did ask them to stay with her, and there's far

13

more room there. As it is, Wilhelmina's had to move into *my* bedroom, and it's no joke. What with her thrashing about and practising swimming strokes in her sleep, it's no wonder I'm getting bags under my eyes. (I don't feel at all well!)

I would have gone to church this morning, Lord, but I'm feeling just a bit narked with you. Besides which, that new vicar leaves a great deal to be desired. Whoever heard of a churchyard where goats and sheep run about free?

What happened last week was downright disgusting. It's common knowledge all over Oswaldtwistle that Mary Maguire's best handbag was chewed to shreds by that gormless goat, while Mary was head-bowed deep in prayer. And what about when poor departed Shaggy Bates was placed in front of the altar while all present prayed for the repose of his soul? It's a wonder he didn't rise from his box when that dirty great ram took a fancy to the chrome trestle beneath, mounted it in full view of everybody, and wheeled poor Shaggy halfway down the aisle.

I've withdrawn my church attendance in protest. And what's more, Lord, I'm not the only one who thinks the vicar's got a cheek charging churchgoers one pound each for the hire of a hymn book during services. If you don't want a full scale strike on your hands, Lord, I think you'd best look into it – if you don't mind my saying so. But don't worry if you're too busy to deal with it straight away. I'll keep you posted about what's going on.

There was chaos this morning. First of all, Wilhelmina had a crying fit when she couldn't find her blue gym knickers. 'I wouldn't be seen dead in those!' she moaned when I fished out a perfectly good pair of pink flowered ones. 'They're babyish. I wore them three years ago when I was six . . . and in case you hadn't noticed, I've *grown* since then.'

I don't know how I stopped myself from strangling her. 'Well, at least your *mouth* has grown!' I told her smartly, while turfing everything out of the ironing basket. Her blue gym knickers weren't *there* either.

As usual, the ever-ready Maggie came to my rescue. 'Here they are,' she said, waving a dark blue garment in the air before unceremoniously stuffing it into Wilhelmina's sports bag and propelling both it and the pouting monster out of the door. 'Get off to school,' she said, 'and no peeking in folks' windows on the way!' Then, before Wilhelmina could protest, she shut the door on her.

Later, when we were washing up, she started giggling. 'What's up with you?' I wanted to know.

'Oh, I'd love to be in that changing-room when smarty-pants takes out her blue gym knickers,' she chortled.

'Oh, why's that?' I asked, feeling a wave of horror wash over me.

'Gym knickers be blowed,' she laughed, 'them's my old Land Army bloomers. Like as not they'll cover every little arse in that school, and go twice round the gas works an' all!' I didn't know whether to laugh or cry. But Maggie has such an infectious giggle that we collapsed on each other in a fit of hysterics.

'You'll pay for it when madam gets home,' I gasped,

the tears rolling down my face. 'Oh, Lord!' I was doing my best to look horrified, but secretly loving every minute, delighted that Maggie had taken that little horror of mine down a peg or two.

Neither of us had noticed Tom looking up at us, intent on our every word. 'I'll tell her what you did . . . and that you laughed and laughed about it!' he threatened. He changed his tune, though, when Maggie swore blind she had seen *him* swap over the knickers in Wilhelmina's bag. 'I never!' he protested, his big brown eyes filling with tears and his voice trembling (he's also suffered at the hands of his horrible sister).

He and Maggie came to an understanding. 'You keep your mouth shut, and so will I,' she said. (Judging by the look on his face as they shook hands on it, I don't think he'll ever trust grown-ups again.)

The postman brightened the smile on Maggie's face when he brought us a letter each. I should have been expecting mine, because I'd only just finished reading my stars. 'News from afar may well put you in a panic,' they said. 'Go on, Maggie,' I urged, nervously turning my letter over and over, 'open yours first.'

Maggie didn't need much urging, because you could see the letter was from the Council. 'They've sent me a reply to my application,' she cried excitedly. 'I bet they're offering me and Ethelbert a house.' Tearing it open, she rushed to the bottom of the stairway, shouting, 'Ethelbert darling, get yourself down here. There's a letter from the Council.' Then to me, with a cocky smile, 'I told you it was a better idea to move in with you, Jessy. They *have* to house you when you're overcrowded, don't you see?' (Personally, from the dealings *I'd* had with them, I couldn't believe they had to do *anything* if they didn't want to.) 'Apart from which,' she added in a whisper in case Ethelbert might overhear, 'although I'm fond of Sonya, I could never live in the same house with her . . . she's so slovenly!'

Her painted-on eyebrows disappeared up and out of sight when Ethelbert paused at the bottom of the stairs to remark, 'Y' don't 'ave ter whisper, lass. It ain't no secret that my daughter-in-law's a tirrible 'ousekeeper. She must be the only woman in the 'ole of England who can go for a month wi'out washing a single pot nor pan.' On seeing Maggie's face screw up in disgust, he laughed out loud. 'After a time yer gets used ter bits o' month-old porridge mixed in wi' yer scrambled eggs . . . an' if you've never 'ad tapioca in rabbit stew, yer ain't lived!' (That's our Sonya for you!)

When we were all settled quietly, Maggie opened the letter and began to read. '*Dear Mrs Potts, Thank you for your most recent communication regarding the allocation of Council houses in Casey's Court.*' Here Maggie gave a sigh of satisfaction and a smug little grin, before Ethelbert urged, 'Go on, go on, lass!'

Patting his knee in too intimate a manner for old-age pensioners, she continued to read aloud: '*And, in particular, your application to rent the recently vacated No. 3.*' (That's right next door, where the marathon-bonkers lived before being evicted for endangering the foundations with their over-zealous activities.)

'What's it say, lass?' cried Ethelbert, getting so excited that his wig slipped down over one eye and his knees began to tremble. (I don't know whether it was excitement about getting their own house, or the fact that Maggie kept grabbing him, but he was growing pinker in the face by the minute.) Maggie had to pause in her reading so he could rush out to the backyard for a quick visit to the lavvy.

Before Ethelbert came back, Maggie sneakily read on. As I watched, the contents of the letter became painfully obvious and Maggie's face went through a whole series of frightening contortions. Just as poor Ethelbert staggered in at the back door, she let out such a powerful roar that he promptly turned tail and took refuge in the lavvy again. 'The rotters!' she cried, rushing to the sideboard to fetch her tin hat. 'They've turned us down . . . turned us down!' There was no consoling her as she marched up and down the room, striding out with her two fists in the air and the battered relic from World War One rammed so tight on her head that her ears stuck out like jug-handles.

'Calm down, Maggie,' I said, watching my precious ornaments doing a frantic jig on the sideboard. (Y'know, I think those marathon-bonkers *have* undermined the foundations.) 'Sit yourself down. I'll make us all a fresh pot of tea, and we'll discuss this sensibly.' (When Maggie gets into one of her militant moods, she frightens the hell out of me.)

'Hey! What's all the uproar?' came the familiar tones from the passage doorway. Was I glad to see that vulgar, short-skirted, big-bosomed figure as it swaggered its way into the parlour, where it sat its shapely bottom into the armchair, crossed its long slim legs and patted its strawberry-blonde head with long crimson finger-nails. 'I could 'ear you buggers from right up the street,' it said, sweeping its long sticky eyelashes from me to Maggie, then back to me. ''As there been a bloody murder or what?'

'Look here, Sonya . . . just you look at this,' moaned Maggie, coming to a halt long enough to thrust the crumpled letter into Sonya's outstretched hand. 'They'll not get away with it, I can tell you. Oh, no! They've not heard the last of this . . . not by a long shot.' (I don't

18

think the Council folk know what they've let themselves in for.)

Sonya, however, was not very sympathetic. 'I telled yer, didn't I?' she said, trying hard not to look like the cat that got the cream. 'They're not gonna give you two old 'uns a place . . . yer could drop dead any minute. Then they'd 'ave ter start all over again.'

That was an unfeeling and hurtful remark to make, and I told her so in no uncertain terms. Maggie was not so kind. She fetched Sonya such a clap on the ear that it knocked her cross-eyed. 'You hard-hearted bugger!' Maggie shouted. 'Give us *your* place, why don't you, eh? You come and move in with Jessy.'

God, what a terrible thought. I visibly sagged with relief when Sonya jumped up holding her burning ear and telling Maggie straight, 'I'm not moving in with anybody, Maggie Potts. I've got me own place an' that's the way I like it. There ain't no need fer you an' yer old fella ter be squashed up an' overcrowded . . . 'cause there's plenty o' room wi' me . . . I've telled yer afore.'

'Move in with you? I'd rather live in Fred Twistle's pigeon-loft.'

'Oh aye? Well, fancy bloody pants . . . 'appen that's just what yer might *'ave* ter do, 'cause the Council ain't gonna give you two a place, I'm tellin' yer!'

There they stood, the two of them, stiff and angry, eyeball to eyeball, Sonya's ear throbbing bright as a beacon and Maggie's chin jutting out so far that you could hang your coat on it. 'You just wait till your pa-in-law finds out what you said,' threatened Maggie.

'Our Ethelbert!' sneered Sonya, flashing her sticky lashes towards the back door. 'If I know that one, he's cowering in the lavvy till the all-clear.'

Thank God for little Larkin from next door. 'Are you

19

opening today, Jessy?' came the thin voice through the letter box. 'I've come for my trim and set.'

It was just the excuse I needed to defuse what looked to be developing into a very nasty situation. 'Off you go, Sonya,' I said, getting to my feet and coming between the two of them, 'you open the shop and make a start. I'll be along in a minute.'

She glowered her brown panda eyes at me. Then, looking from me to Maggie, she gave out a great roar of laughter, at the same time slapping her hands on Maggie's shoulders. ''Ark at the pair of us, Maggie darlin' . . . fallin' out an' screamin' at each other. An' us such grand old friends, ain't that right?'

To which Maggie reluctantly nodded her tin hat, saying with a grin, 'Aw, Sonya, I'm sorry I belted you one, honest.'

'Naw, gal . . . I deserved it, me an' me big mouth.'

So peace was restored and all was forgiven. 'But there's still a score to settle with the Council!' declared Maggie, putting on her coat. After which she dragged poor Ethelbert from the lavvy, and the pair of them went away up Casey's Court, to do war with the world.

Tom protested just as loudly when I marched *him* up the street for his first day at school. 'I'll run away!' he said. (Promises, promises.)

'I hope he's going to make a more well-behaved start than your Wilhelmina did,' remarked Mrs Hepher, the headmistress. 'Do you recall what upheaval she caused when she first came to us?' (Could I ever forget!) 'Go on, Mrs Jolly,' she told me, 'go quickly . . . just leave him with me. And don't look back.'

I could hear him screaming as I hurried away, and when I got to the corner I heard him shout, 'You don't love me!

That's why you've given me away. Well, I don't love *you* either!' (Please yourself, I thought.)

I'm sorry if I'm not a fit mother, Lord. I did explain how I felt about kids, and you still went ahead and gave me two to look after. So I can't be blamed, can I?

Tuesday, January 10th

Maggie's been sulking all day, because the Council flung her and Ethelbert out. 'I did warn you,' I said, in an effort to calm her down.

'With all due respect, Jessy,' she retorted with admirable dignity, 'I'd be grateful if you'd shut your gob!' Then she dragged Ethelbert off to confront the local MP.

I'm quite pleasantly surprised at how Tom has taken to school – like a duck to water. 'I like Mrs Hepher,' he announced. 'She loves me, and I want *her* for me mum instead of you.'

Wilhelmina looked up from her comic to pin him with one of her grown-up no-nonsense stares. 'Don't be silly,' she told him firmly, with a shake of her long fair hair, 'teachers don't love *anybody* . . . it's not allowed.'

'Who says so, Miss Know-all?'

'Who d'you think, clever-clogs . . . the authorities, of course!'

Tom ignored her irritating habit of rolling her brown eyes heavenwards and throwing up her hands in despair. 'You're a liar, then,' he yelled, ''cause she *does* love me. She says I'm a little gentleman. An' if you don't believe me, I'll kick you in the arse!'

I had to intervene at that point. 'I've told you before, Tom,' I said, 'we don't want that sort of language here!'

Then he looked me straight in the eye and moaned in a

21

tearful voice, 'If Sonya says it, so can I. And Mrs Hepher does love me. She *does*!'

'Of course she does,' I lied.

'Hmh!' declared Miss Mouth Almighty. 'Why don't you ask her to adopt you, then, eh? Ask your precious Mrs Hepher to take you home with her for good.'

He was sobbing fearfully now. 'She *will* an' all! She *will* take me home for good, if I ask her.' (I should be so lucky!)

I had a strange experience in the salon today. A man came in just as I was trimming Smelly Kelly's moustache. (He's so clean and smart these days I reckon he's got himself a new girlfriend.)

''Ere, that fella's tekken a fancy to you, Jessy,' he remarked with a sly grin, when I took his money at the counter.

'Don't be so daft,' I said, turning a bright shade of crimson, and pretending not to know which 'fella' he was talking about.

'Go on with you!' he chided. 'He ain't took his eyes off you this past twenty minutes or more. An' I've seen you peeking at him when you thought nobody else was looking.' I gave him his change quickly, and shoved him out of the door.

He was right, though. And Sonya had noticed it too, because she kept tittering and winking at me every time she turned him round in the chair to clean up his neck. I was so embarrassed I would have made any excuse to escape. But the woman from the tripe shop was waiting for a cut and set and Marny Tupp from the Barge Inn needed a quick back and sides. Every time I glanced up, the bloke in Sonya's chair was staring at me. Really nice-looking he was, as well; not too tall and generously filled out, with thick light brown hair and cheeky dark blue eyes that spoke volumes . . . as if he knew a secret and I didn't. When at one point I caught his eye I went all silly and jabbed the scissor-points in Marny Tupp's earhole. 'Christ Almighty!' he yelled, leaping three feet into the air. 'Are you trying to cut both sides from one bloody end, or what?' After that, I kept my eyes on the job, and even resisted the urge to peep when I heard Sonya closing the door behind her mysterious customer.

After the salon was shut up, we had a little chat about him. 'Took a real shine to you, gal,' she laughed. 'The poor bugger was besotted. D'you know, every time he opened his mouth, it were to ask about you . . .'ow long 'ad you been in Casey's Court? Where did you come from? Were you spoke for? What was yer name?' She was thoroughly enjoying it, I could see. 'An' weren't 'e the most darlin' little fella ye've ever clapped eyes on, eh? Them navy blue eyes! Oh, I'm tellin' yer, Jessy . . . that one's a little sweetie, yer can see it a mile off. Pity about that battered old van 'e drove off in, though, eh?'

On and on she went, until, seeing I wasn't going to be enthused by it all, she said cheerio and went off home – just as Maggie and Ethelbert returned with news that our local MP was going to take up their case with the Council. 'You'll see the fur fly now,' Maggie said. I wasn't too hopeful for her, but I said nothing, because the last thing I wanted to do was to discourage her, bless her old heart.

The kids kept on about what Sonya had so foolishly allowed them to hear. 'If this bloke fancies you, like Sonya says,' remarked Miss Know-all Wilhelmina, 'why don't you go out with him instead of that Barny Single-ton?' She never has taken to Barny.

''Cause she don't want to, that's why!' piped up Tom. 'And if she does, I'll tell Barny on her.' (Sweet little thing!)

23

Ten minutes later, when they'd both had the quickest lick-over in the history of child-washing, I marched the pair of them off to bed. 'And don't let me hear another peep out of you,' I said, turning out the lights.

'Who's this fella they've been on about?' asked Ethelbert, grinning from ear to ear as Maggie's teeth sank into his neck. 'Gerroff, you silly thing!' he giggled, turning the other cheek.

'Yes – this fella,' said Maggie, dragging herself away from his stubbly wrinkled flesh, 'who is he?'

After I described him, from those dark blue eyes right down to the old van that he drove off in, Ethelbert asked a question which I must admit had occurred to me. 'What were the fella doing round these quarters, eh? An' coming to a little back-street barber's to gerr'is 'air cut?' Ignoring the 'back-street barber's' bit, I told him that I had been wondering the same thing.

'Yes, and what was he gawping at you for . . . and asking Sonya all them questions about you, eh?' murmured Maggie, a troubled look on her face. ''Tain't the Council up to their old tricks, is it?' (She does have a thing about the Council, does Maggie.)

I assured her that he didn't look like any Council official I'd ever met, and that seemed to satisfy her to a point. 'Then who the hell was he?' came the cry from Ethelbert. And that's just what I'd like to know.

I was woken in the early hours by a terrible screaming, followed by a burst of insane laughter. It didn't worry me, though, because I recognized the voice as belonging to one of Sonya's 'clients'. Oh, well – whatever turns you on, eh?

Wednesday, January 11th

Another busy day. Had a lovely evening out with Barny
. . . candlelit dinner and soft talk. It was just the tonic I
needed. He really is gorgeous, what with that shoulder-
length midnight hair and those black sexy eyes that can
turn me to butter. He has a way of making you feel really
special. Funny thing, though. It's been over a year since I
turned him down when he tried to coax me into a sexual
encounter of the third kind. He hasn't asked me since.
And I believe I'm ready to take the plunge – but *I'm* not
lowering myself to be the one to approach it. When I
foolishly mentioned it to Sonya, she knew the reason
straight away. 'He's gerrin' 'is oats elsewhere, gal. An'
ye've only got yersel' ter blame!' she said. (I can't
understand Barny at all sometimes.)

Thursday, January 12th

Unusually quiet day. Closed the salon at noon.
   Maggie and Ethelbert took the horrors to the pictures,
while Sonya and I went off to the sales in town. I got
myself a lovely pair of red high-heeled shoes and a bag to
match, for only a tenner the lot. Sonya stocked up with
eye make-up. And she bought a long buckled leather
thing from the saddler's. 'What do you want that for?' I
asked, quite puzzled. 'Whatever is it?'
   'It's best you don't know,' she said, 'then if yer ever
tortured, they can't mek yer confess, can they?' When I
shook my head in confusion she added with a chuckle,
'Look 'ere, Jessy gal, all yer need ter know about this 'ere
thing is that it'll give some lucky bloke nightmares fer
bloody weeks!' (It doesn't bear thinking about.)

25

The real excitement of the day came when we wandered into a china shop. I've never seen so many shelves upon shelves of beautiful bone china, and all at half-price. 'Cor bloody Nora!' said Sonya, trudging through the place like the proverbial bull. 'Mek a powerful crash if this lot went, wouldn't it, eh?' When she swung round to make sure I was following in the crush of bodies, some unfortunate little woman who was foolish enough to be within firing-range of Sonya's 44D cups was sent reeling. In a minute the place was in uproar. Somebody shouted 'fire' and there was a panic-stricken surge for the door. In the confusion, row after row of porcelain jugs were sent clattering to the ground, and three floor-hands were trampled underfoot.

I'm not surprised that Sonya was singled out by the manager. It was stupid of her to stand by the door jumping up and down with glee and shouting, 'Smile . . . yer on candid camera!'

Friday, January 13th

Unlucky for some. Certainly for poor old Fred Twistle whose entire flock of racing pigeons escaped. 'Yer bloody gormless twerp, Bertha!' You could hear the commotion from one end of Casey's Court to the other. 'I've telled yer afore, pigeons ain't like dogs . . . yer don't let the buggers out fer a walk!'

Back came the curt reply to 'Sod off . . . you *and* yer mangy birds!' Then a door slammed, and five minutes later Fred was seen running up and down with a great big net on a stick. (I feel ever so sorry for him.)

I had a bit of panic of my own when Ethelbert and Tom went out to give old Fred a hand. Tom ran back in all excited and breathless. 'Quick, Mam,' he shouted, 'I've seen her again.'

'Seen who?' I asked, thinking he wanted me to help capture old Fred's best breeding hen.

'That film star in Barny's parlour! Come on . . . come and see for yourself.'

I didn't need telling twice. 'You get off, Tom,' I told him, 'and help Fred to retrieve his birds.'

Hoping there was nobody watching, I crept along the wall from Barny's front door to the window, careful not to make a sound. If he *was* carrying on behind my back, I had a right to know, and woe betide him. Just as I was stretching my neck to peer into the parlour window, little Larkin emerged from her house with bucket, cloth and whitestone. On seeing me, bent double beneath Barny Singleton's window, she looked quite taken aback. 'Are you all right, dearie?' she shouted at the top of her voice, causing a nosy upstairs window cleaner to almost tumble from his ladder. 'Visiting your sweetheart, is it? Ah, that's nice.' I could see her puzzling as to why I was crouched beneath the window instead of knocking on the door like any normal human being. I daren't open my mouth in case Barny and his spare bit were warned off. Instead I gave a weak, watery smile, and waved my hand as I cautiously backed towards the door. (If I looked as foolish as I felt, both she *and* the window cleaner must have thought me three bricks short of a load.)

'Ooh, look!' cried Larkin, beside herself with excitement and blasting off from both ends. 'He's at the window.' Sure enough, there was Barny, nose squashed to the glass and eyes swivelled in my direction. Little Larkin had spoilt everything.

In a minute the front door was flung open to reveal the gorgeous Barny bedecked in scarlet dressing-gown and

27

looking deliciously tousled. 'Jessica!' (He *had* been up to no good, I could tell.) 'Goodness me, have you been at the door long, darling? You should have banged a bit harder.' (See what I mean?)

'Oh, I did,' I lied, 'I made enough noise to raise the dead . . . were you having a nap?'

He took me by the arm and invited me in – which confused me, I can tell you, because I was convinced the 'film star' was hiding in there somewhere. Inside, I took mental note of everything. The parlour gave nothing away, because all was exactly as when his old mother had been alive . . . except for a tiger-skin draped over the sofa. I mentioned to Barny how out of place it looked against the heavy walnut furniture and the wooden rocking chairs. He laughed, saying, 'It's just one of my little perks.'

While Barny was upstairs getting dressed (I wasn't invited) I searched the back parlour and scullery. There was no sign of the 'film star' and the back door was still securely locked. The bugger's upstairs, I thought. And when Barny came down, I pretended I needed to go up and visit the loo. 'Off you go, then, sweetheart,' he said, giving me a devastating smile. 'I'll make us both a cup of coffee.' He wasn't a bit bothered, and so innocent did he seem that I nearly changed my mind. But there was something going on here – I could feel it.

Whoever little Tom saw, or *thought* he saw, she must have made herself invisible . . . either that, or Barny had flushed her down the loo, because I searched all three bedrooms, every cupboard, and even *under* the beds. But there was no sign of her. I once saw a James Bond film where the other woman was hanging from the window sill by her finger-tips, so I opened all the windows and looked out – nothing! My first thought was to run downstairs and throw my unworthy self into Barny's arms. My second thought was to leather Tom's backside till he couldn't sit, for telling such mischievous lies. And I might have done *both* were it not for my third thought. There was a most distinctive smell in both the bathroom and Barny's bedroom. A heady and overpowering scent of expensive perfume. And while we were drinking our coffee Barny was fidgeting and on edge, apparently in a hurry to get rid of me. By the time he was seeing me to the door, I had worked up enough courage to ask him outright. 'Barny, are you two-timing me?' There was no other way to put it.

He seemed devastated that I should even think such a thing. 'Jessica Jolly,' he murmured, blowing in my ear, 'I would never do that. *You're* the only woman I want.'

'Well, if that's the case, why haven't we named the day?' (I couldn't believe my own boldness.)

He had no real answer to that. 'I've only just got my divorce through, Jessy, and it's all been such a draining experience . . . what with her having taken my son to the other side of the world. Look, sweetheart . . . be patient. When I feel ready to take the vows again, there's nobody I want to be standing beside me but you.' (God, he's a charming rogue is Barny Singleton.)

'If you *are* seeing another woman, though, or if you want to end our relationship, Barny . . . don't be afraid of hurting me, because I'd rather know.' I wasn't fully convinced that he was telling the whole truth. But he went out of his way to assure me that there was nothing further from his mind than another woman. So, for the time being anyway, I've given him the benefit of the doubt.

Sonya thought I was a fool. 'There *is* some'at bloody funny going on, Jessy gal. An' I for one am gonna keep me eyes peeled. If I find out the worm's having it off wi'

29

some scrubber, 'is sodding feet won't touch the ground!'
(I didn't say anything else to Sonya, but . . . I can't help
wondering why Barny didn't take the opportunity to drag
me into bed. I'm beginning to feel desperate. When it
does happen, I'll have forgotten how to do it!)

Saturday, January 14th

It's my thirty-seventh birthday today. I took a good long
look at myself in the mirror this morning, and it put me
in a state of panic. Tom was right about the 'squiggly
lines' round my eyes, and not only are they getting deep
as tram lines, but they're spreading! And I've put on at
least four pounds, and it's all settled round my hips. I'm
beginning to look like one of those round-bottomed toys
that roll about when you flick them with your finger. Like
a fool I mentioned it to Sonya. 'There y'are then, gal!'
she roared. 'It's like I told yer, darlin' . . . yer ain't
gerrin enough. What! There ain't nowt like sex to keep
yer slim.' When I said cattily that sex hadn't done much
to reduce the size of her bosom, she took great pleasure
in pointing out that while bounteous hips were an ungainly
sight, a woman's charlies were more attractive to men if
they were big, bouncy and beautiful. 'Besides, the fellas
like somewhere ter rest their weary 'eads when they've
done their bit.' (I'm fed up now.)

Maggie's had a letter from the local MP. 'He's coming
to pay us a visit this Friday,' she shouted, hugging poor
Ethelbert till his eyes nearly popped out. (As it was, he
only just managed to catch his false teeth in his tea cup.)
'*He'll* get us the house next door, I know he will.' She was
walking on air all day. I do hope she's not going to be
disappointed.

30

It was a quiet day in the salon. Saturdays are never all that busy, so I asked Sonya to cut and restyle my hair. Now it's short, sharp and chic. I went out and bought an exercise bike to do the same for the rest of me. (Tonight I managed a quarter of a mile at four miles an hour.)

Barny took me out for a drink to celebrate my birthday. He wanted to take me for a meal, but I told him I was on a diet. 'I like you the way you are,' he said, giving me the sort of squeeze that tells the world about your spare bits. 'I prefer a woman with a bit of padding on her.' (Sonya must be right, because, according to Tom and Wilhelmina, Barny's 'film star' is well padded up top.)

'You haven't changed your brand of aftershave, then?' I asked, sniffing round his collar.

'No, why do you ask?' he wanted to know.

'No reason,' I lied, not forgetting that distinctive smell of expensive scent in his bedroom.

Isn't it funny . . . once the germ of suspicion is sown, every harmless comment becomes sinister. So when he said 'I may not be seeing you for the next few days, because I'm considering going to the hairdressers' convention', I was convinced he was really off for a bit of how's-your-father with the buxom beauty. Liar, I thought, quietly seething. What I actually said was, 'Oh, I'd go myself . . . but I think it's a waste of time.' (I forgot to tell him I hadn't been invited).

We had a bit of a scare after we'd all gone to bed. (But at least it finally solved a little mystery which occurred soon after we moved here from the south.) Ethelbert raised the alarm, and almost gave me a heart attack when he came charging into my room after midnight, his nightshirt flapping round his nether regions, the broom handle in his mitts and our Maggie bringing up the rear in her new psychedelic curlers with her faithful tin hat

31

perched on top. 'Evacuate this room!' Ethelbert yelled (and oh, he did look comical without his teeth in. His mouth was like a black hole and his whole crinkled-up face seemed to have fallen into it). 'Gerrout!' When I hesitated, thinking it was some sort of nightmare, he jabbed me with the broom handle.

'Have you gone daft or what?' I mumbled, half asleep.

'Gerrout, I tell yer. There's somebody trying ter get in the front door, an' like as not they'll mek fer this bedroom window when they find the door bolted agin 'em.'

'That's right, Jessy,' cried Maggie, already pulling the reluctant Wilhelmina from beneath the bedclothes. 'Me and Ethelbert crept downstairs when we heard the scrabbling at the door, and we couldn't see a thing through the letter box. Y'know, I think it's the same fella as tried to get in once before. D'you remember . . . when I threw that brick into the night and mad Aggie fell in the door?'

'Aye, that's right, Jessy . . . *I* remember right enough. Pissed as a newt, weren't she?' sniggered Ethelbert. (He's really frightening when he laughs without his teeth in. For a moment there I thought I'd be sucked away for ever.)

He shut up, though, when Maggie sharply reprimanded him. 'Don't you make fun of the dear departed,' she said. (Poor Mad Aggie performed her last cartwheel over the cobbles on Christmas Eve, when she collided with the Salvation Army's Jesus waggon. I'm surprised, Lord, that you didn't see it coming and arrange a detour. Still, I expect you needed Mad Aggie up there to entertain the angels, eh?)

'Never mind about Mad Aggie,' said the shivering Ethelbert, 'everybody gerrout of 'ere – go on!' He propelled us towards the door, where Tom had appeared, looking more bewildered than I was.

'What's Grandad Berty doing?' he asked.

He started to whimper when back came the answer from the Black Hole, 'I'm saving us all from being slaughtered in us beds, that's what! There's a bad 'un trying ter get in. But the bugger's in fer a shock if 'e shows 'isself at this window . . .'e won't be so bloody confident wi' a six-foot broom handle stuck up 'is arse!'

What followed will remain in my memory for many a year to come. After we'd all been herded downstairs and Ethelbert took up guard by my bedroom window, Maggie and I crept along the passageway – I armed with the poker and she with a pair of coal tongs. 'Force yer way in here,' she warned the would-be intruder, 'and I'll have your balls between me prongs!' (I was saying nothing. What *could* I say?)

Anyway, there we were, up against the door and trembling every time a scratch came from outside. 'Have you rung the police station, Maggie?' I whispered, gesturing to Tom and Wilhelmina to get back and stay in the parlour. (Lucky didn't need any telling, the cowardly dog. I could see his terrified saucer-eyes peering out from beneath the sideboard.) When Maggie said Ethelbert had told her not to ring the police 'because yer don't need nobody else when you've got me', I lost no time in tiptoeing back to the parlour to ring the local station.

'There's somebody trying to get in,' I told the duty officer in a frightened voice. It was my favourite helmet – the faithful bobby who had seen us through thick and thin and who, because of adverse and unfortunate circumstances beyond my control, was convinced that I was the most evil, corrupt and wanton woman since Eve.

'Oh, it's you again!' He was *not* overjoyed to hear from me. 'Are you *sure* there's somebody trying to get in, Mrs Jolly? I'm *not* saying you're imagining it . . . but I haven't forgotten the last time you dragged me out for the same reason. You do remember the occasion, I take it?' I reminded him that what happened to Mad Aggie was not our fault. After all, she gave us more of a fright than we gave her! Besides, there *was* someone trying to get in that night. And he was back again!

'All right, all right, Mrs Jolly, calm down. I'll be along straight away.' (He sounded enthusiastic, I must say.)

'Don't break your neck getting here,' I told him, slamming down the phone.

Suddenly all hell was let loose! From the front door came the jubilant cry: 'I've got the bugger. Tell Ethelbert to come quick!'

As I raced towards the stairs, shouting, 'Quick! Maggie's got him through the letter box with her coal tongs!' Ethelbert came crashing down with the broom handle.

'Gerrout the way, Jessy!' he yodelled as the tip of the broom handle wedged itself up his crutch. The commotion put the fear of God into Lucky, who shot out with his tail between his legs and launched himself full speed up the passageway.

'Bloody Nora!' yelled Maggie as Lucky thudded on to her stooping shoulders. 'The bugger's jumped in through the fanlight!' Whereupon she lost all caution and flung the door open. Out shot the cowardly Lucky . . . and our Ethelbert, who was charging down the passageway with his broom handle going before him. The poor constable never had a chance. Lucky sailed through the air to land on his helmet, and Ethelbert – broom handle and all – careered into him with such force that the wind was knocked clean out of him.

By this time half the street had tumbled from their beds to investigate the rumpus. There wasn't one upstairs window without a body hanging from it. 'Shut thi' bloody

34

noise!' shouted the woman from the tripe shop. 'Decent folks is trying to get some sleep!'

'I'd be over to give you a hand,' called Barny, 'but I can't find my slippers anywhere.'

'I'll have the lot of you thrown in the cell!' shouted the helmet from beneath the tangle of arms, legs and dog paws. 'Especially *you*,' he yelled in my direction. 'Yer a bad influence on this street . . . I've said it afore.'

'Ye've let the bugger escape, yer gormless sod!' Ethelbert yelled. 'Yer as much use as a rag doorknob!'

Once everybody had struggled to their feet, red-faced and sore, it was all I could do to stop myself laughing. 'Right then,' declared the angry helmet, taking out his pencil and note-pad, 'inside, the lot of you. This is all going down in my report.'

No sooner had we all trooped back into the passageway and closed the door than there came a scuffing and knocking from outside, while the letter-box flap clattered up and down as though somebody was trying to open it. 'Ooha,' gasped Maggie, throwing herself around Ethelbert, 'it's him again!'

At once the helmet took charge, dissuading the courageous Ethelbert from taking his damaged broom handle and ramming it through the letter box where he might make a lucky strike. 'No, old fella,' he said, 'you take yourself off upstairs. I'll tackle it from down here, and if all else fails you can jump on the scoundrel from a great height.'

'I bloody will an' all!' promised Ethelbert. (You have to admire the silly old fool.)

What a night! The upshot of it all was that Maggie developed a nervous rash; Ethelbert worked himself up to such a frenzy that we had to enlist the helmet's assistance to restrain him; Lucky peed on the new mat;

and the kids had an all-out fright. The 'culprit' trying to force an entrance turned out to be a mangy moggy who used to live here, and the helmet threatened to take me to court for wasting his time.

On top of everything else, I caught sight of a big, buxom woman with high heels and masses of black wavy hair. She was walking on the far side of the road, and when she saw me staring at her she hurried away out of sight. It worried me, because she exactly matched Tom and Wilhelmina's description of Barny's 'film star' . . . *and* she was coming from the direction of his house. But I can't be really sure of it, so I daren't tackle him. I'll watch him like a hawk from now on, though. (I think I've got piles.)

Sunday, January 15th

I couldn't get up this morning. I woke up feeling inadequate, and I couldn't find the courage to face the world.

Sonya took it upon herself to take charge. She kept flitting in and out of the bedroom with hot drinks and lurid descriptions of her perverted sex life. 'We'll have you feeling like a spring lamb in no time at all,' she assured me, leaning over to pat my pillow straight. (Not only was I temporarily blinded by having my face squashed into her cleavage, but I seemed to have taken a turn for the worse.) 'Look here, gal,' Sonya told me later, 'if yer not better in the morning, don't worry, 'cause *I'll* look after yer customers.'

(Funny how I suddenly felt fit as a fiddle.)

Monday, January 16th

Ethelbert and Fred Twistle went to a pigeon sale today. When Maggie voiced her protest at Ethelbert's leaving her, he gave her a bit of flannel. 'Now then, Maggie, old darling,' he said, sliding his arm round her and pecking her on the cheek, 'absence meks the 'eart grow fonder, they say . . . though I can't see me loving yer any more than I do now.' She fell for it, hook, line and sinker, and watched him and Fred Twistle toddling off up the street like a couple of geriatric Bisto kids.

'Y'wanna watch that old fella o' yours, Maggie,' warned Sonya in her usual indelicate manner. ''E's my pa-in-law . . . so I know a bit more about 'im than 'e cares to admit. Oh aye! Yon Ethelbert Pitts were a randy bugger in 'is day. An' they do say as 'ow a leopard can't change its spots.'

'Give over, Sonya,' I said, seeing how she was upsetting poor Maggie. 'Ethelbert's too old for that sort of thing . . . "randy", indeed! There comes a time when a man is past it.'

Maggie was not pleased. 'Too old!' she scoffed. 'I can assure you that my Ethelbert is far from past it.' Then she added more quietly, 'Though he may not have enough to share it about.'

I think we must have set her thinking, because she slunk about all morning looking sullen and concerned. At two o'clock, after the last perm had been despatched and things had gone quiet in the salon, she said to Sonya and me, 'You two take yourselves off to town. Go on . . . I can manage if any last minute customers turn up.'

I knew she could. And I also knew that she wanted to be on her own. 'All right, Maggie,' I said, trying to look grateful, but feeling guilty for having teased her about

Ethelbert. 'That's very thoughtful of you, and to be honest I've been meaning to take those red shoes back. They aggravate my corns terribly.'

'Good idea,' rejoined Sonya, taking off her smock and putting on her coat. 'I 'ave ter go to the chemist, 'cause *I've* got a complaint!' (I daren't ask.)

'There's no way you're getting *me* to come into the chemist's with you,' I told her, 'not after last time!' (She had put the place in an uproar, picking and choosing from the display of condoms and asking advice from all and sundry.)

'Gerroff!' she roared, pushing me playfully on the shoulder and sending me reeling against the sideboard. 'Yer too bloody sensitive, gal. What's more, I picked up two clients from the queue that day!'

In town we went our separate ways, she to the chemist and I to the shoe shop. The arrangement was that I would change my shoes, then come to the chemist's to meet her. After that, we would go to John Lewis for a cup of tea and a prawn sandwich. I'm very partial to prawns. Sonya claims that's why I'm so besotted with Barny Singleton. But I think she's just jealous.

The manager of the shoe shop gave me a really hard time. 'I'm sorry, madam,' he snorted, 'these shoes were in the sale, and we don't change sale items.'

Well, I soon put him in his place. I told him: 'There are laws to protect people like me. I'm a consumer, and as such I have certain rights.' He was a jumped-up little jerk, who seemed to know the book of rules as though he'd written it himself. But I wasn't going to let him get the better of me. So we argued for a while, and though he did seem to be in the right *I* came out on top. When I walked out of that shop with a pair of gorgeous blue sling-backs, my head was held high. (It was only when I got home that

I discovered they were size three, and I take a five. Sonya's right. I am a 'silly cow'!)

I swear I'll never go into town with Sonya again. Sitting on the flower tub outside the chemist, I could hear Sonya's voice: 'Extra long? They're *never* extra long! I doubt if ye've ever seen an extra long one in yer bloody life! Just *look* at 'em! I've a good mind ter 'ave yer under the Trades Descriptions Act!'

When she came bouncing out, I rushed her away through the gathering crowd, my face going every shade of scarlet. 'Honestly, Sonya . . . do you *have* to show yourself up like that?' Then she rounded on me. (I suppose it's right enough what she says, though. It *is* her that takes the stick from dissatisfied clients.)

After queuing for what seemed an age, we finally struggled into the lift at John Lewis. I was ready for a sit-down and a welcome cup of tea, but when we were halfway between floors the lift got stuck. 'Bloody Nora!' moaned Sonya. 'What next?'

It was ages before anybody came. A leather-clad spotty-faced youth began to get really agitated. I do believe if it hadn't been for Sonya's intervention he might have caused real panic . . . eight of us squashed in as we were. At one point he really scared me by flinging himself at the door and screaming, 'Lemme out! Or I'll *smash* me bloody way out!' When Sonya fetched him one round the ear he slumped into a corner, whimpering like a baby until we were rescued. After that he got to his feet, stuck out his chest (and two fingers to Sonya) and sauntered off as if he was a hero or something. 'Uncouth lout!' yelled Sonya. 'Cocky as arse'oles and thick as bloody sick!' (Put me right off my prawn sandwich.)

At five minutes past midnight, Ethelbert and Fred Twistle came rolling home, drunk as lords – though

Ethelbert put it more crudely when Maggie angrily flung open the door to let him in. 'I'm pissed as a newt,' he chortled, his legs buckling under him as Maggie knocked the cap from his head.

'Don't you talk to me!' she said angrily, marching upstairs. It was agonizing, lying there and hearing poor Ethelbert stumbling about and staggering into everything.

'Yer a wicked woman!' he kept shouting, after which he would burst into a garbled version of 'We're a couple of swells'. When he did finally manage to reach the top of the stairs, he turned the wrong way and came tumbling into *my* bedroom.

'Look at him, he's horrible!' mumbled the sleepy Wilhelmina. 'Get Maggie to take him away.' (I had to admit he made a frightening sight, swaying against the door, with the light from the landing silhouetting him like a ghost.)

'Maggie!' I shouted, clinging to Wilhelmina. 'Come and fetch your Ethelbert!'

Back came the curt reply, 'No, I won't. Throw the swine back down the stairs!'

With a sigh, I got from the bed and propelled him carefully along the landing. 'You've lost your way, Ethelbert,' I said.

He promptly gave me a loud and jolly rendering of 'My old man says follow the van and don't dilly-dally on the way. I dillied an' dallied, dallied an' dillied, lost me way an' don't know where to roam'. Then he banged on Maggie's door, pleading, 'Let me in, yer bugger. I've gorra surprise for yer.'

Maggie told him firmly, 'You can stick your surprise *up* the chimney! *I've* got one for *you*: I've bolted the door and it's *staying* bolted!' Whereupon he fell in a bedraggled heap and fell fast asleep. (Dear Lord, please get them that house next door. I fear for my sanity.)

It was three A.M. when finally I got to sleep. I covered silly Ethelbert with a blanket before creeping back to bed, then I lay shivering for ages, listening to Fred and Bertha Twistle going at it hammer and tongs up the street. I heard 'And bloody well *stay* out!' from Bertha and 'Yer '*eartless* . . . '*eartless*!' from Fred before the door slammed shut. A few minutes later he found his way to our house.

When I opened the window to tell him to stop shouting for Ethelbert, he doffed his flat cap in a most gentlemanly fashion, looked up, and told me in an apologetic voice, 'I might look a sketch, because I've 'ad a drink or two, Jessy, gal. But I've been chucked out bag an' baggage. Oppen' door, there's a good 'un. Me bloody arse is freezing!'

I can hear him snoring down on the sofa. Oh, there's going to be some singing and dancing tomorrow, I'll be bound!

Tuesday, January 17th

What a day! Sonya was trilling at the top of her voice about how wonderful life is. 'Oh, Jessy gal,' she laughed, 'I really look forward to me Monday night sessions with Danny Dent. There's never a dull moment, I can tell yer. First 'e wants dowsing down with chocolate milkshake, then 'e wants ter 'ang upside down with 'is ankles mana-cled. Oh, it's exciting! Ye've no idea the things 'e comes up with!' (I have. I have.)

At half-past eight this morning Bertha Twistle fetched her Fred. 'He'll rue the day he ever met me when I've finished with him!' she promised, propelling him out of the door by the scruff of his neck. Fred took it well, even though he was stricken by a riveting hangover.

'Do yer worst, Bertha Twistle,' he told her. 'I'm a man of stern quality, an' I'm proud ter say I wore a uniform fer King an' country during the war.'

'Huh!' retorted Bertha. 'You silly old fart! Some uniform you wore, eh? There's nowt to be proud of in being a lavatory attendant when your pals are on the front line!'

Fred was furious. 'Shut yer gob, yer daft sod. *I* did my bit. I stood my ground when bombs were dropping all about me.'

'Aye? Well . . . there's bombs . . . an' "bombs",' she said callously as they disappeared from sight.

Poor Ethelbert looked like something the cat dragged in. He stood at the bottom of the stairs, all bent and withered, with bloodshot eyes and trousers at half-mast. (I can't understand why Maggie will insist on buying his trousers from the boys' section in Woolworths. I know it's cheaper. But even when she's let the hems down the legs are *still* too short. It looks as if he's jumped into them too far. And I have to be honest . . . he is not a pretty sight at the best of times.)

'She won't talk to me,' he complained, slurping down the cup of tea I made him.

Feeling sorry for him, I had a word with Maggie. 'He's suffered enough,' I said, 'and you know he'll not do it again.'

'No, he won't!' she retorted. 'I'm stopping his treats . . . that'll teach him!' (Whatever next? And him coming up to seventy!)

42

I had a letter from Tiffany today. She went on and on about how she missed me after all those years of living next door to each other. 'I have no friends here at all now, Jessy,' she wrote, 'not since you left, and I'm very lonely.' It is a shame, bless her, because she was the only one who stood by me when I was widowed and penniless. Now, since her husband left her for another woman, she seems to be falling apart. I've asked her on several occasions to come and stay with me. But she won't. 'I couldn't bear it up there,' she says, 'all those foreign Northerners and poky little houses.' I've already explained how I felt the very same way when I had to move here. And now I wouldn't go back south for the world. 'Ah, well, Jessy,' she argues, 'you were never on the same social level as me, were you, dear? So it was probably easier for you to adjust.' In spite of her loneliness, I've got a feeling that Tiffany will take a long time before lowering herself to pay Casey's Court a visit. Maggie's taken a positive dislike to her.

'Tiffany,' she scoffs, 'what sort of a name's *that*? If you ask me, she's a toffee-nosed yuppie, and we don't need her sort round here!'

I've got a dreadful cough. No doubt from wandering about the house in my nightie at all hours. After the salon closed, I decided to go to the doctor's surgery. 'You want to steer clear o' that dirty ol' sod,' warned Sonya. ''E's got some funny ideas.'

'What do you mean . . . "funny ideas"?' She had me worried.

'Well, for a start 'e's outlived three wives. An' I'll bet yer a tenner that 'e'll ask ter examine yer arse.'

I was disgusted and told her so in no uncertain terms.

43

'Is nothing sacred to you, my girl?' I demanded. 'All doctors have the highest professional standards which you should respect.'

'Huh!' she retorted. 'If you mean that there whatsits-name . . . hypocritical oath, well, it's a load of bullshit if yer ask me. I'm telling yer, gal . . . that Dr Petal's a randy ol' bugger. Why d'yer think *I* go to him?'

'His name is *not* Dr Petal. And he comes highly recommended, so I'm taking no notice of you whatso-ever,' I told her.

All the same, thanks to Sonya's teasing, I did feel slightly apprehensive when the receptionist ushered me into the aged doctor's surgery. He seemed a nice enough little chap, with his light blue eyes and semi-bald head. 'Hello, Mrs Jolly,' he smiled, 'it's nice to meet you at last. Now, what seems to be the matter?' He had a pleasant soothing voice which put me at my ease straight away. I told him about my sore throat and the irritating cough. He was most attentive and concerned. (So much for Sonya's warning.) The consultation was over in no time at all. (It might have lasted a bit longer if he hadn't instructed me to take my clothes off and lie on the couch.) I shall write to Buckingham Palace about it. The Queen will know what to do.

There's some other funny business going on as well. I've had a letter out of the blue from a solicitor in town. Apparently, he has been instructed by his client to make an offer for my house and salon. It really shook me up. 'It's that Maggie Thatcher!' declared Sonya. 'She's 'eard 'ow well yer doing, an' she wants it fer 'er Denis.'

Maggie came up with a different speculation. 'It wouldn't surprise me at all if it wasn't that crafty Barny Singleton. He's been itching to get his hands on this place,

44

ever since we first came here. The bugger can't stand the competition!'

She set me thinking, because just lately when I even *mention* the salon to Barny, he changes the subject. And I know he can't be too pleased that a lot of his old customers now come to me. I phoned the solicitor and asked him who his client was, but he wouldn't give me any information, other than to say that his client wanted to remain anonymous. When I put it to him point blank that I thought it was Barny Singleton, he said that there was nothing further he could tell me, and would I inform him as soon as possible regarding my decision about whether to sell. I gave him my answer there and then: 'I have no intention whatsoever of selling my home and business.'

'I will convey that information to my client. But if you change your mind, please let me know at once.'

I can't get to sleep for thinking about it. And when I stormed over to confront Barny Singleton, he was most upset to think I should accuse him of 'such a back-handed thing'. (But he didn't take me to bed to console me!)

'Don't you believe a word he says,' retorted Sonya and Maggie both. 'He's out to get these premises. And what's more, the bugger's two-timing you with his dark-haired buxom beauty. You can bet your pants on it!' I don't know *what* to think any more.

Thursday, January 19th

Wonderful news! Maggie and Ethelbert have had a letter from the Council, and they've been allocated the house next door. 'Good ol' gal,' chuckled Ethelbert, slapping a

45

wet and rubbery kiss on Maggie's cheek. 'I *knew* ye'd do it, yer little beauty.'

Maggie wallowed in the praise, but was quick to point out that it was all down to the local MP who had taken up their case with the Council. 'Come on, Ethelbert, chichi-coo,' she said, putting on her coat and taking him by the hand. 'Let's go and tell him how grateful we are, eh?'

As they toddled off up the street hand in hand, Sonya and I watched from the doorway. 'Ah, just look at the poor little sods,' she cooed affectionately. 'Yer can't 'elp but love 'em, can yer, eh?' She was right. They made such a pathetic and loveable sight . . . Maggie with her four-inch heels which kept throwing her legs apart, and all lopsided as well, because one of the shoulder pads was missing from her coat. And Ethelbert, his flat cap rammed so tight on his head that his ears looked like helicopter landing pads and those schoolboy trousers fanning out from the top of his sock-suspenders. 'If anybody ever 'urt 'em,' Sonya choked, her eyes all misty, 'I'd swing for the buggers!' (I know just how she feels.) We began to plan a house-warming party for when they move in.

Friday, January 20th

I do wish Maggie wouldn't go on so much about her love life. She's making me quite envious, although I suspect she does exaggerate a bit. I can't really believe that old Ethelbert pranced across the cowfield and 'chased me into Cockey Spinney. It was two o'clock when we went in, and we didn't show our faces till three hours later.'

'Huh! If I know Ethelbert, 'e showed yer more than 'is bloody face!' chortled Sonya. 'An' did 'e tell yer 'ow Cockey Spinney was 'is favourite place as a lad? I'll bet the old fox didn't tell yer that Cockey Spinney was where 'e first 'ad a bit of 'ow's-yer-father!' (She does have a colourful way of putting things, does our Sonya.) It was obvious she was teasing Maggie and trying to wind her up. But Maggie refused to be offended.

'You can say what you like, Sonya Pitts,' she said indignantly, 'I love my Ethelbert . . . and I'm not the slightest bit concerned about *what* he did before we met!'

But Sonya wasn't giving up that easily. 'They do say as 'ow the woman from the tripe shop is the result of one of the old bugger's orgies down Cockey Spinney! Who knows *'ow* many middle-aged folks are walking about, not knowing they've gorra fart like 'im for a dad? An' did the randy old sod tell yer 'ow 'e got Molly Mauls in trouble down Cockey Spinney, eh? I bet 'e forgot to mention *that*, when 'e 'ad yer drawers round yer ankles!'

Maggie showed nothing but contempt for Sonya. 'You ought to be thoroughly ashamed of yourself, Sonya Pitts!' she said, taking out her hankie and blowing her nose as though she hadn't a care in the world. 'Fancy sullying your own pa-in-law's character like that!' (She even made *me* feel ashamed, and I hadn't said a word!) She walked off with such dignity I was proud of her.

'Cor, stone the crows!' exclaimed Sonya. 'She won't believe nowt agin 'im, will she, eh? The sun must shine out of 'is bloody arse!'

It was three o'clock this morning when I finally got to sleep. Maggie was shouting things like 'Of *course* it's true, if Sonya says so!' and 'Who *were* all these women you had your way with down Cockey Spinney?'

She sounded furious. I think it was silly of Ethelbert to yell out, ''Ow the bloody 'ell am *I* supposed to remember 'em all? I never bothered ter ask their names!'

I wasn't at all surprised when she flung him on to the

landing and locked the door against him. 'Let me in, else I'll 'ave yer up afront o' the human rights court!' he protested.

'Go on, then!' shouted Maggie. 'I'll have *you* pickled as a specimen and put on display in the museum!' (That shut him up!) 'And what's more,' she went on, 'I've a good mind to tell the Council I don't want the house next door. There's no telling whether I'm safe with a nymphomaniac under the same roof.'

'What the 'ell's a "nimfimanic" when it's at home?'

'Somebody who can't control his urges, you dirty old bugger!'

'Well, *I* ain't one o' them, matey . . . 'cause I'm doing all right controlling the urge ter burst this 'ere door down an' give yer bare arse a bloody good smackin'!'

'See what I mean, you sex-monster!' yelled Maggie, dragging a heavy article across the floor and ramming it up against the door. 'First thing tomorrow, I'm getting a divorce!' There then followed a long dark silence, until the heavy article was shifted again and the door creaked open. Maggie's voice said in an embarrassed loud whisper, 'You wouldn't *really* give my bare arse a good smacking, would you?' I couldn't hear what Ethelbert's reply was. But the two of them shuffled back into the room amidst much tittering and sniggering – followed by little shrieks of delight from Maggie.

'Mam,' mumbled Wilhelmina from beneath the bedclothes, 'what's Maggie and Ethelbert fighting about?'

'Their rights,' I said, pulling the clothes over me and feigning sleep. Well, I'm *past* sleep now. And me at that delicate age when I need all I can get. (Yes, that too!) Roll on when I'm old. I'll probably have much more fun.

We were run off our feet in the salon today. On top of everything, I was ordered by Sonya to give a running commentary on what took place last night. 'It's all *your* fault,' I told her. 'It was thanks to you that I didn't get much sleep.'

'Well . . . hush my mouth!' she chuckled, doing a cheeky little dance as she took off her smock. Lord knows where she gets her energy from, because I feel as though I've been through the wringer. At least Sonya did little Larkin's wash and set, thank goodness, because my aching head couldn't have survived being in such close proximity to the dear little soul's rear end. As though reading my thoughts, Sonya laughed. 'Little Larkin was in good voice today, weren't she, eh?' Then she related a couple of smutty jokes told to her by Smelly Kelly. 'Funny thing,' she said, referring to her recent short relationship with the same fellow, 'you'd never credit such a gurt big lump as that with 'aving such a pathetic little thing. I told 'im there were certain exercises 'e could do to improve on it. But 'e musta been frightened, 'cause 'e ain't been around since.' (Judging by the screams which often emanate from Sonya's bedroom, I can't blame the poor chap.)

'We're not all partial to torture!' I told her.

Later on, I had a visit from Barny. 'I'm sorry if I've been neglecting you lately, Jessy,' he said, 'but I've had such a lot on.' (And a lot off, I thought, with the dark buxom beauty in mind.)

I assured him that he mustn't give it another thought. I wish I could put him out of my heart, because he does cause me a deal of anxiety – what with my suspicions about the woman who's been seen by all and sundry, and the solicitor's letter asking me to sell up. It's all very

49

worrying, and though Barny denies any involvement on both counts, I can't bring myself to believe him. And I can't prove he *is* involved – either with another woman or with a devious plan to get me out of house and home. I keep trying to forget how dead set he was against me when we first came up here to open the salon. He tried everything he knew to shut me down, because I was threatening his own livelihood. I've said all this to his face, but he assures me it doesn't matter any more, because he loves me. But if what he says is true, why doesn't he ever actually make love to me? And why is he so nervous whenever I mention marriage? Also, I've had no real sense out of him regarding the expensive perfume I smelled in his bedroom that night. If he's lying to me all along, then all I can say is he's the most convincing liar that ever walked. I wish I could give him up altogether. But he only has to look at me with those gorgeous dark eyes, and I'm lost.

Seeing how down I was, he insisted on taking me out for a candlelit dinner at the Rose Inn, where I could 'relax and forget the wear and tear of the day'. And, to my surprise, all the weariness melted away from me once I was sitting opposite him, the soft glow bathing his handsome features and his fingers entwined with mine. 'You look lovely, as always,' he murmured, in that caressing silky voice which makes me go weak at the knees. Afterwards, he only had to say the word, and I would have done *anything* for him. For a minute, when he drove me to his unisex salon to show me the new luxurious refurbishment, I really thought it was going to happen. He whispered in my ear, turning my legs to jelly. Then he slithered my coat to the floor and took me in his arms. He kissed me in a way I've never been kissed before, and my heart was leaping somersaults as he gently bent me backwards over his newly-installed Italian marble counter. (It struck cold to the nether regions but I was past caring.) This is the night, Jessy old girl, I told myself, pouring everything I had into his arms. But the moment was shattered when all of a sudden there came a spooky whirring noise, followed by a piercing whistle, then an agitated female voice crying, 'I gave it a good rubbing, and I showered it down with lather and hot water, but it's *still* this ghastly purple colour! I shall be on your doorstep first thing in the morning, Mr Singleton. And if you can't satisfy me, I'll consider it my duty to write to the Hairdressers' Federation!'

After switching off the offending answerphone he made a half-hearted apology, drove me home and didn't even kiss me goodnight as I climbed out of the car. It was almost as though he'd been pleased at being interrupted before doing something he might later regret. I can't fathom it out for the life of me, and I don't know what to do. (I've decided not to tell Sonya about the incident, because she'll only say something crude.)

Sunday, January 22nd

I had intended to have a lie-in this morning. But Tom woke up screaming in agony. (Kids have no consideration whatsoever.) Feeling it my duty to take him to the doctor's, I made an urgent appointment for nine-thirty A.M. I particularly asked for a lady doctor, but there was only Sonya's 'Dr Petal' on call on a Sunday. 'He's so good with children,' cooed the dopy receptionist. (At least *I* was safe. He wouldn't dare ask to examine my bottom, not with little Tom in tow.)

We were in and out in no time. 'What's up wi' the poor

little bugger?' Sonya demanded to know. When I told her, she ran into the scullery on the pretext of brewing a pot of tea, but I knew she'd really gone in there for a good laugh. When Maggie came downstairs looking the worse for wear, Sonya couldn't wait to relate the news. 'Little Tom's been bawlin' all night,' she told Maggie (whose sleep had also been disturbed), 'an' Jessy's just back from the doctor's with 'im. Poor mite.' She lowered her voice and pulled a face. ''E's got a fistula up 'is arse!' She also pointed out that 'arses' were Dr Petal's speciality, and that he never lost an opportunity to ''ave yer bloody drawers off an' stand yer on yer 'ead'. We were then treated to a vivid and mind-boggling account of how one of her clients suffered from the very same weakness.

'Good grief!' exclaimed Maggie, suddenly wide awake. 'Does he still come to you?'

'Not bloody likely!' retorted Sonya. 'When I 'old a conversation, I likes ter look in folks' *faces* . . . not be confronted wi' a bunch of dangling doodahs. I do 'ave me standards, y'know . . . in spite o' what's said about me!'

It was a real performance putting the ointment up Tom's poorly. (I could never thread a needle either.) 'What's the matter with Tom?' demanded Miss Bossy-boots. 'I expect it's just an excuse to have a week off school.'

'No, it's not,' protested Tom. 'I've got a fishtilly . . . and it really hurts!'

'Hmph!' Lady Know-all was not impressed. 'I bet you've only got piles,' she said. 'Billy Shetter's mother's got them. When *she* sits down, Billy says she's got to sit all lop-sided because they prick her, and she's. always complaining that only somebody else with blistered piles can possibly know the agony she's going through. But Billy says she's a softie, because if he had blisters up his bum he'd stab them with a fork, and then they wouldn't be no trouble no more.'

She really upset Tom. Now he's terrified of turning his back on her in case she comes at him with a fork.

Whoever said Sunday was a day of rest never lived in *our* house!

Monday, January 23rd

That man turned up again today . . . the one who eyed me in that peculiar fashion while Sonya was cutting his hair some time back. This time, though, he didn't come into the salon. He just drove slowly up and down Casey's Court. Twice he pulled up outside the window to peer in at us. "Ow do,' shouted Sonya, waving her arm with such enthusiasm that she knocked Florrie Humble's glasses clean off her nose. 'Cor, bugger me, gal, I'm that sorry!' said Sonya, fishing them out of the sudsy water in the basin and wedging them upside down on Florrie's nose. 'Never 'ad much use fer spectacles mesel',' she chuckled proudly.

I must say my curiosity's aroused, though. As Sonya says: 'Who the 'ell is that bloody fella? An' what's is interest in *you*, gal? Because 'e's gorris eye on yer, an' there's no use tryin' ter deny it.' She's right. He certainly does seem very interested in *something*, but whether it's me or Sonya's overpowering cleavage there's no way of telling . . . not without *asking* him, anyway. And that's just what I intend to do the next time he shows his face round these quarters. (It won't be difficult, either, because he's got a nice friendly face. The sort that makes you come over all motherly. And that's a rare experience for the likes of me.)

53

Talking of experiences, there's one in particular that I'm really looking forward to, and that's the house-warming for Maggie and Ethelbert. They've to go down to the Council offices and collect the keys tomorrow morning. Oh, they're so excited! Like a pair of teenagers. 'Just think, Ethelbert my chichicoo,' Maggie giggled. 'We'll have our own little love-nest at last.' He came over all daft, took her by the hand and crept away upstairs with her. (I'm really jealous! I can't wait to be old and wrinkled . . . then *I* can be somebody's 'chichicoo'.)

Tuesday, January 24th

I'm not likely ever to forget the day Maggie and Ethelbert were due to collect their keys from the Council. They went off down the street arm in arm, tails wagging with excitement. Maggie got over-emotional and shed a few crocodile tears before she departed. 'Oh, Jessy, just think! Me and my Ethelbert with our own little hideaway,' she sniffled, blowing her nose on the corner of my smock. 'Won't it be fun choosing the furniture, eh?' She was quite beside herself.

We've made arrangements to visit Tipples' warehouse some time in the next few days. We're bound to pick up a few choice items of furniture there. Tipples is the local rag-a-bone man. A colourful character, with long matted ginger hair springing from beneath a chequered flat cap, merry green eyes which seem always to be laughing, and a large loose mouth full of small, even, snow-white teeth. His baggy ravelled jumper dangles to his knees, which jut out from the ragged holes in his trousers, and his over-large plimsolls turn up at the toes. If ever there was an eccentric, it's Tipples Rafferty, a loveable rascal who hates to be trapped within four walls, and loves his 'pint o' the best'. He can be heard many a time, coming up the street on a dark night, drunk as a lord, his 'foine voice' giving a splendid rendering of 'When Irish eyes are smiling', and his old horse pulling its comical load across the cobbles in what can only be described as a dangerously haphazard fashion, for, being as generous as the next fellow, Tipples makes it his bounden duty to share the spoils of his life with that faithful animal. A commendable and generous trait, which includes the fair sharing of his 'pint o' the best'. A body can never tell who's had more over the eight . . . Tipples or his old faithful! There's only one thing to be sure of. When you hear Tipples' song, sung in a particular way, and the waggon wheels playing a peculiar tune on the cobbles, get out of the way just as fast as ever you can!

Still and all, Tipples is loved by everybody. He has a heart of gold, and a monstrous affection for the old brown mare who has pulled his painted waggon these past twenty years and more. 'When my old faithful goes to the knacker's yard,' he tells one and all, 'I'm going with her.' But if he loves her, then it's no more than she adores him.

'Y'know, Jessy,' Sonya said to me in an unusually serious voice one day, as Tipples and his colourful painted ensemble passed the window. 'The likes of old Tipples Rafferty is a dying breed. When 'e's gone, it won't ever be the same round these 'ere parts.'

I was surprised to see Sonya in such a quiet mood. I was even *more* surprised when Ethelbert told me later that Tipples and Sonya were lovers a long time ago. 'Serious, they were. Then she met and wed my worthless bloody son, and Tipples ain't never forgiven 'er.' I was under the impression that beneath all those rags and whiskers Tipples was much older than Sonya. 'Naw . . .

'e ain't above forty-two, an' 'e ain't never loved anybody else since Sonya.' Ethelbert was also of the opinion that Sonya still loved Tipples, 'though she'd never admit it. It's *pride*, gal. Pride as keeps 'em apart . . . Tipples being bitter at 'er choosing another, and Sonya being afeared ter go after 'im in case 'e tells 'er ter piss orf . . . which I expect 'e *would* do an' all. Who could blame the feller, eh?'

As I gazed after Tipples and his rickety old flat-waggon, I could sense the quiet thoughts running through Sonya's mind. Trying to distract her, I said I'd never before seen such a sight as Tipples and his rag-a-bone cart. It was certainly a rare and astonishing sight as it meandered away down Casey's Court. There was the waggon, its great wood and iron wheels painted a myriad of bright swirling colours, and the sides of the cart itself festooned in rolling waves of pink and blue, with carpets of green and white flowers painted between. It's a real glimpse of the past, a rare nostalgic sight, and a glory to behold. 'One of these foine days, me ol' beauty,' he's been heard to tell the aged mare, 'Oi'll point yous along the road to the Emerald Isle, an' we'll spend us days wi' the little leprechauns sure we will.' Like all of us, Tipples has a cherished dream, which may never come true. (Mine is to catch Barny and his buxom beauty red-handed!)

By the time we closed the salon at five o'clock, there was still no sign of Maggie and Ethelbert. 'I expect they've got the key,' said Sonya, 'an' the buggers 'ave gone down Cockey Spinney to celebrate.' (She does have a one-track mind.) I was a little concerned that they hadn't come straight back, as I knew Maggie was itching to get inside her new home and go through it from top to bottom with a scrubbing brush. Still and all, as Maggie was fond of telling me, they *were* old enough to please themselves what they did. And, as Sonya pointed out when she rushed off home to see to one of her 'clients', 'Maggie wouldn't thank you fer frettin' o'er 'em, gal. 'Cause when all's said an' done, they're past gerrin' in trouble, aren't they? I mean . . . 'tain't as though they're a pair of irresponsible yuppies, is it, eh?'

It was gone midnight when they rolled home, drunk as skunks and stretched out on the rag-a-bone man's flat-waggon. 'Oi found these two staggering down Cobbler's Alley,' explained the bemused Tipples, himself the merrier by a pint or two of the best. 'Sure they ain't safe ter be out on the streets, I'm tellin' yer. Especially not when the ol' fella me lad was banging on every door along the way, telling folks how the Council were coming ter chuck everybody out on the streets.

'Best leave 'em where they are,' he advised, once we had Maggie on the sofa and Ethelbert in a chair. 'Be Jaysus! They must 'a sunk a gallon each,' he roared, taking a last look at the pair of them. And I had to agree. Maggie was out to the world, her face all blotchy and one of her painted eyebrows having disappeared altogether. Ethelbert wasn't much better, either. Both his wig and his flat cap had slid over one earhole, his flies were undone, and his bottom set was resting on his chin. 'Looks like they enjoyed theirselves, though,' laughed Tipples as he went down the passage, 'celebrating their new home sure an' all.'

I covered them with blankets before coming to bed. 'Oh, Maggie,' I told her, taking off her shoes and making her comfortable. 'You'll pay for it tomorrow, darling. I wouldn't want your hangover for all the world.'

To my surprise, she stirred, opened her eyes and began to cry. 'I want my little house,' she sobbed. 'You promised! You told me I could have my own little love-nest.

Liars! Liars, the lot of you!' Try as I might, I couldn't get any sense out of her, so, leaving her be, I fetched myself upstairs before the kids came down. I wouldn't want them to see Maggie and Ethelbert in such a state.

I can't sleep, though. What did Maggie mean when she called out, 'You told me I could have my own little love-nest. Liars, the lot of you!' Surely the Council haven't gone back on their word about letting her have the house next door? No . . . they wouldn't do that. They *wouldn't*. (I've got an awful feeling in the pit of my stomach. I expect it's the wind. I *hope* it's the wind.)

Wednesday, January 25th

Well, it's all happening! And none of it good. When I came downstairs this morning, it was to find Ethelbert and Maggie gone. A quick search told me that they had managed to drag themselves up to bed some time in the night. There they lay, bless their old hearts, tucked up beneath the clothes, hands held on the bedspread and both sets of false teeth side by side on the dresser. They were both obviously fully dressed . . . Ethelbert still had his flat cap on. Well, *nearly* on, because, together with his wig, it covered all of his face – with the exception of his mouth, which was wide open and emitting snores to wake the dead. Maggie was facing him and sucking his earhole. 'Aw, poor little buggers,' said Sonya, having come upstairs to gaze at the culprits. Once I'd related the time and manner of their arrival home, she was on their side. 'At *their* time o' life, Jessy gal,' she said, 'there ain't much pleasure left in this 'ere world. So go easy on 'em when they crawl downstairs, won't yer, eh?' When I told her how Maggie had cried, and what she'd said, Sonya was in no doubt as to the reason for it. 'Them bloody Council wallahs 'ave done the dirty on 'em,' she roared, 'you see if I'm not right. I bet they ain't lerrin' Maggie an' Ethelbert 'ave that 'ouse after all!'

She was *partly* right, as we discovered when Maggie staggered down the stairs, eyes all red and sticking out like hat pins, and every slight noise sending her into spasms. 'Serves yer right, yer drunken sod!' exploded Sonya in a merry fit, before being discreetly despatched to the scullery.

'Go and make us all a strong brew,' I told her.

In painful whispers, Maggie then related how the keys to next door had been withheld because of 'unforeseen circumstances'.

'What bloody unforeseen circumstances?' Sonya wanted to know. (So did I, but I was less noisy about it.)

Anyway, according to Maggie, she had insisted on an explanation as to why they were not being given the house keys. 'I told them straight . . . me and my Ethelbert were not budging from their office till we knew exactly what was going on.'

'I bet the capitalist sods 'ave *sold* it, ain't they? I bet that bloody Maggie Thatcher's told 'em ter sell it!' (She has an unhealthy dislike for our Prime Minister, has Sonya.)

'No, it isn't that,' Maggie told her.

'What then?' I asked, concerned that poor Maggie and Ethelbert had been cheated out of their 'love-nest'. Maggie said she didn't know, because all the Council would tell them was that the house at No. 3, Casey's Court, had still to be inspected. And that, when the Council was fully satisfied, she and Ethelbert would be given the keys . . . they need have no fear about that. Maggie had pointed out that the house had *already* been

59

inspected, because she herself had seen the workmen departing it. Finally they asked her and Ethelbert to leave.

'They clammed up,' Maggie finished, 'and wouldn't tell us another thing.'

Later, when she and Ethelbert were better recovered from 'drowning their sorrows', they toddled off down the street, full of plans to see the local MP again. Ethelbert was in two minds. 'Won't the fella be sick of us keepin' worrying 'im?' he asked Maggie.

'Ethelbert Pitts!' she cried, giving him a scathing look. 'Where's your spunk, my man? You must *never* lose your get-up-and-go, or the faceless ones will tread you into the soil!' (She could be a poet, could Maggie.)

Going to the MP wasn't much help. 'Well, it wouldn't be, would it?' declared Sonya with disgust. 'Not when 'e's buggered off to Turkey fer a month's holiday!' So there's nothing to be done but wait and see what transpires. We're all going to keep a close watch on next door.

'What!' declared Maggie, getting ready her tin hat. 'There won't be a mouse getting in or out that I don't know about!'

Tom and Wilhelmina have set about building a camp in the backyard of No. 3. 'I'm in charge,' said Tom. 'I'm big and I can flatten anybody who tries to get in.'

'I'm in charge, dumbo,' said Wilhelmina. 'I'm *bigger* . . . and I can flatten you!' (She's right!)

I'm so tired, I've gone past sleep. And the noise from little Larkin's room next door is quite deafening. 'Oh, Mam!' moaned Wilhelmina, emerging from beneath the covers. 'I wish Larkin would stop farting! I can't get to sleep.' (That's Sonya's influence again. I shall have to have another stern talk with her.) But Wilhelmina's quite right, when all's said and done. If only little Larkin could control her sorry affliction, we might *all* get some sleep. Instead, I can hear Maggie and Ethelbert stirring, and then little Tom, all sleepy and frightened.

'Can I sleep with you, Mam?' he wanted to know from the doorway. 'The thunder's frightening me.'

Wilhelmina put him right. 'That's not thunder, stupid,' she smugly informed him. 'It's that Larkin farting again!' (Don't you just love them to death.)

Leaving the brats arguing, I joined Maggie and Ethelbert downstairs, where we sat till dawn, supping tea and putting the world to rights. 'We should be grateful for small mercies,' I said. 'At least we haven't got the marathon-bonkers banging away all night on the other side of us.' (Mind you, judging by the soppy way Maggie and Ethelbert keep gazing into each other's eyes, we might be in for an even *worse* fate when *they* move in next door!)

'I shouldn't be at all surprised if that little house wasn't *made* for lovers,' mooned Maggie, gently stroking Ethelbert's bony knee, 'don't you think so, chichicoo?' (I'm convinced I must have been wicked in my past life. Why else is my cross bigger than everybody else's?)

Thursday, January 26th

It's been a disastrous day! First of all, one of the hairdriers exploded while the woman from the tripe shop was under it. 'Hell bloody fire!' she yelped, springing out and diving for cover. 'Are yer trying ter finish me off, or what?' Sonya was no use at all, so while she was doubled up in fits of laughter at the sight of the poor woman cowering terrified under the bench with her rollers smoking I ran to

61

the stairs cupboard and switched off the mains. (I can be a real hero when the occasion warrants it.)

A strong cup of tea and a double-decker soon calmed the poor thing. 'My God!' she said after she'd stopped shaking. 'That quite put the wind up me, I can tell yer. I thought I'd be blown to kingdom come!' (Sonya was quick to point out how it was a good job little Larkin had just left, 'or we might *all* 'ave been blown to kingdom come!') It *was* frightening, though. I'm glad Maggie and Ethelbert were out picketing the town hall, because I've got a feeling that Ethelbert's like me – his nerves are going!

'Seein' as 'ow the salon's out of bounds while the wiring's being attended to, let's you an' me go into town, eh?' suggested Sonya. 'We can have a bite to eat an' do us shopping, instead of gerrin' trampled underfoot tomorrer night.' Thinking it a splendid idea, I promptly agreed, and made a few apologetic phone calls to those who were booked in for today. While I was doing that, Sonya put together a notice for placing on the window to inform any passing trade.

'Don't frighten them,' I warned her, 'or make them think it's anything untoward. Just say we're closed due to an emergency, and we'll be open as usual tomorrow.'

She was most affronted. 'D'yer think I can't be discreet when I want to?' she snorted. It was only after we were on our way down the street that I glanced back to read the large childish print scrawled over the window in scarlet lipstick. I was horrified to read:

WE'VE HAD AN ACIDANT WITH THE ELECTRIKS. SO WE DARN'T HAVE NOBODI IN TODAY, IN CAIS THEY GETS THERE HEDS BLOWN OFF.

(Needless to say, we'll be going shopping tomorrow night. It took over an hour to remove all traces of the lipstick, and anyway, I'd rather be 'trampled underfoot' at Sainsbury's than be put out of business.)

Friday, January 27th

There was a little row this morning. Maggie wanted to drag Ethelbert down to the Council offices at seven-thirty. 'Don't be so bloody daft!' he protested. 'What's the use o' picketing the place when it's empty? There'll be nobody there till gone nine, woman.'

Maggie wouldn't be put off. 'That's just it,' she explained with surprising patience, 'we shall catch them going in. They'll not be able to hide behind their venetian blinds *then*, will they, eh?' (How could he argue with that?)

'Well, I don't intend standing there freezin' and starvin',' he told her. And, give the old soldier his due, he wouldn't move till she'd packed him half a dozen banana butties. 'A fella like me 'as ter keep 'is strength up,' he told her, flexing his muscles, 'else 'ow am I supposed ter keep *you* satisfied?' (The mind boggles.)

The salon won't be open until tomorrow now. 'Your wiring's falling apart,' the electrician informed me. 'I don't know how it's held together till now.' (If I can do it, I'm sure the wiring can!) 'You need some new cabling and a modern junction box,' he said, all the while eyeing Sonya's heaving cleavage. 'I'll have to go and collect a few things from the stores. But I can fix it up temporary so you can brew up and the like.'

While he was doing that, Sonya was draped all over him, the consequence being that he wired everything up wrong. Lights were going on and off, the toaster was turning somersaults, and every now and again we got a flash of 'How to do it in twelve different positions' on the TV screen. 'Can we stay at home from school and watch the bonkers on telly?' asked the kids, all boggle-eyed. (My piles are playing me up now.)

Sainsbury's was packed. Three times Sonya had somebody run into her legs with a trolley. 'I'll raise this bloody roof if it 'appens agin!' she screamed. 'Can't the buggers see where they're going, or what?' I begged her to calm down and keep out of their way. ''Ow the 'ell can I keep out o' their way, yer silly cow,' she wanted to know, 'when the sods come at me from be'ind?' (Hush your mouth, Jessy gal, I thought – there's trouble brewing.)

Sure enough, Sonya exploded. But it was nothing to do with trolleys attacking her – although that got her all riled up to begin with. It was when we got to the check-out that the real trouble started. When it was her turn, there was a queue a mile long behind us. 'Bloody Nora,' moaned Sonya, 'it's worse than the charge o' the Light Brigade!'

Anyway, everything appeared to be going smoothly. She had nearly finished, and I was preparing to unload *my* trolley when she slapped the last item on the belt – a delicious blackberry pie, topped with cream and beautifully packaged. 'We'll enjoy that wi' a small lager,' promised Sonya with a wink and a grin. The grin became a frown when the check-out girl discovered there was no price tag on it. At once, she rang her bell and held the pie in the air, trying desperately to catch the eye of any passing assistant (she did look pink and flustered, poor little thing). Behind us in the queue we could hear moaning and complaining, and to dispel the growing murmurs I turned about, dispensing smiles and making small conversation. At last a supervisor appeared, took a look at the offending article and toddled off to get the

64

price. Meanwhile, several trolleys at the back of the queue went and attached themselves to the end of another line, and the remaining ones began to fidget and chatter as their owners began to tremble.

'The weather's not bad for this time of year, don't you think?' I asked one and another, the smile slipping from my face beneath their frozen hostile stares.

'Tek no notice of 'em!' instructed Sonya, drumming her fingers on the conveyor belt and making the check-out assistant somewhat nervous. Every now and then she'd stretch her neck to see whether the supervisor was on her way back. 'Where the 'ell's she gone?' demanded Sonya. ''As she fell down a bloody 'ole or what?'

'It's *your* fault!' shouted some irate woman from the back. 'You should make sure that you get one with a price on it. But I expect your bloody tits are so big they get in the way, is *that* it?'

'They'll not gerrin the way if I come back there an' smack you one in the gob!' yelled Sonya, waving her fist and growing redder in the face by the minute.

'Calm down, for heaven's sake,' I told her, between smiling at one and all.

'It's allus the bloody same!' shouted a new voice. 'Yer allus get *one* silly arse who holds everybody up.'

'Aye, you're right,' rejoined another, 'and I shan't be coming here on a Friday again . . . not now I know Dolly bloody Parton does *her* shopping on a Friday.'

'Come on, you up front! Gerra sodding move on. D'yer think we've gorrall night, or what?'

'Shut yer moanin' cake 'oles!' yelled Sonya, stretching her neck to glare down the queue. Of a sudden, she caught sight of the one doing the most complaining. 'It's *you*!' she shouted, charging past me and knocking folks out of the way like nine-pins. '*You're* the clumsy git as crashed yer trolley into me legs!'

Within minutes the place was in uproar. Everybody was scuffling to get a punch at everybody else. There were all manner of articles flying through the air. I caught a grade 2 egg in the back of the neck; the poor check-out assistant was lambasted with one of Sir Matthew's 'bootiful' turkeys, and a poor old fellow who was waiting for his wife got a pound of best mince between his legs.

I could hear the frantic announcement going out over the Tannoy: 'Please leave the store in an orderly manner', it said, until someone whizzed a tub of cream cheese at the speaker, after which it became slightly garbled. The check-out assistant and I couldn't hear it at all after that – the reception wasn't very clear from where we were, crouched beneath the conveyor belt.

'Is your friend a lunatic?' she wanted to know.

'Yes,' I said, not being one to tell lies.

Eventually the crowd dispersed and the manager appeared. Seeking a full explanation, he was told of the sequence of events leading up to the pandemonium. 'Oh, and what took you so long to get the price?' he demanded of the indignant supervisor.

'I was taken short,' she said, head held high in the face of interrogation, 'and I will *not* accept the blame. Everybody's entitled to go for a leak when nature calls.' (Quite right too!) 'And if I'm to be made a scapegoat, I think it's my duty to tell head office how you take Polly Pickens behind the fruit-and-veg every Saturday lunchtime. And, what's more, I don't give a *bugger* for your authority, because I think you're a right pissant . . . we *all* do! Ain't that right, girls?' she called out to the gathering staff, who seemed to be one hundred per cent behind her.

Quickly now, before she got further involved, I dragged

66

Sonya towards the door. 'Let's get out of here,' I said. 'I think you've caused enough trouble.' She looked like a refugee out of World War Two. Her strawberry-blonde hair was standing up in petrified clusters and her best pink blouse was ripped to shreds.

'You just 'ang on a minute, Jessy,' she told me, pulling free and sneaking back to the conveyor belt. 'Up the workers!' she yelled, grabbing the offending pie and whamming it towards the manager. As he ducked, the supervisor caught it full in the face. At that point I ran.

'There's nowt like a bloody good all-in scuffle, is there, gal?' laughed Sonya, when she caught me up. 'I expect we'll be banned from Sainsbury's now, eh?' (Whatever gives her *that* idea?)

Saturday, January 28th

Tiffany's in a bad way. I've had another pathetic letter from her, and she sounded so depressed that I rang her up the minute I closed the salon. 'I'm going to end it all,' she sobbed. 'Not only has my brute of a husband left me for some inferior woman, but I've just had a letter from his solicitor saying the house has to be sold and the proceeds divided.'

'Look here, Tiffany.' I put on my firmest voice. 'You told me that you'd stopped loving him a long time back . . . isn't that so?'

'Yes, but . . .'

'And you don't really give a monkey's if you never clap eyes on him again?'

'Well, no . . .'

'And you've got no mortgage on that house . . . which incidentally is worth somewhere in the region of one

67

hundred and fifty thousand pounds. Which means that, when it's sold, *your* proceeds will amount to no less than seventy-five thousand pounds?'

'But that's not the point, Jessica! You know as well as I do that seventy-five thousand pounds won't buy a *chicken-coop* down south!' She was crying again. When I suggested that she might do what I had been forced to do and move up north, the crying became hysterical. 'Oh, I could *never* do that, Jessica! I wouldn't fit in with cloth caps, turbans and pigeon fanciers! How could you even *suggest* such a dreadful thing?' She was quite beside herself. But, to be honest, after coming to know and love the very things she despised, Tiffany seemed like a plastic person in comparison to folks down Casey's Court. I made her a proposition.

'Come up here and stay with me for a fortnight. See how *I've* settled in, and meet all my friends. Please, Tiffany.' I could see no other way of helping her. 'Just *think* about it? If nothing else, it'll get you away from Milton Keynes for a while, and we can have a good old gossip about the old days.'

But she was adamant. 'You're not all that sympathetic!' she accused. 'In fact, I do believe you're jealous because I'll come out better than *you* did, when you lost Vernon.'

'Don't be silly, Tiffany. I've offered you the hand of friendship and a place in my home . . . humble though it may be. And it's all I can offer, because the salon only makes enough to keep us comfortable. So you must take it or leave it.' After I'd suffered another of her crying sessions, I had at least wrung a promise from her to *think* about what I said. When I put the phone down, I felt that of the two of us, in spite of the traumatic times I went through before finding a haven in Casey's Court, *I* was by far the better off. Not because I had a fancier house –

which I certainly didn't – and not because I was rolling in money, which I wasn't and probably never would be, but because I had seen the shortcomings and artificial character of the values by which Tiffany lived, and by which I myself had lived not so very long ago.

'D'yer think she'll come?' asked Sonya when I told her about it. 'I 'ope she does, 'cause it's been a time since we saw a toffee-nosed southern git round these parts.' She laughed. 'Oh, but don't you worry none, Jessy gal . . . just leave yer posh friend ter me. I'll soon put 'er right!' (Up till then I'd thought I'd done the best thing by inviting Tiffany to Casey's Court. Now I'm not so sure.)

There's been a great deal of coming and going next door. From eight o'clock this morning we had a never-ending procession of flat-capped workmen and inquisitive important-looking men. There were also a couple of fellows with tripods and sinister-looking equipment traipsing in and out, and thumping the walls with such gusto that Lucky took to the streets like a bat out of hell, and my customers had to shout to make themselves heard. 'Bloody Nora!' exclaimed Sonya, trying to drink a cup of tea and slopping it everywhere. 'Are the buggers tryin' ter knock the place down, or what?'

A terrible thought occurred to me. 'You don't think the Council's pulling a fast one and demolishing the houses as they come empty, do you?' Even I had begun to suspect their every move.

'Huh! We'll soon find out about *that*.' At once, Sonya was out of the door and demanding to know from a passing carpenter: 'What the 'ell's goin' on in there? What are you buggers up to, eh?'

The poor fellow didn't know much more than we did. 'All I can tell you is that when I measured up for the skirting-boards last week, the floor alongside the party wall between the houses seemed to be sinking. But for Gawd's sake, don't let on that *I* told you,' he urged, already fearful that he'd said too much.

'There yer are, gal!' Sonya came rushing back in, breathless and excited. 'I *telled* yer as 'ow all that bloody bonking 'ad weakened the foundations!' Once she'd related to me what the carpenter had told her, there was no holding Sonya. By teatime, everybody down Casey's Court knew. The woman from the tripe shop was certain it was all a ploy to justify pulling down the whole street, and Marny Tupp from the Barge Inn has called a meeting. As for me, I waited till I was on my own, then I rolled back the carpet from the wall between us and No. 3. Sure enough, the floor *is* sinking. (And with it, any hopes I had that we would eventually dissuade the Council from pulling down Casey's Court.)

Later, when Barny came over to take me to the pictures, I saw the side of him that I don't much care for. 'Never mind,' he said, his gorgeous dark eyes bathing my face. 'If they demolish your salon, I'll always give you a job.' As if that wasn't enough, he suggested it might be a good idea if I were to sell him all my equipment now.

Now we've got another problem to contend with. A little while ago Ethelbert and Maggie returned from the town hall, where they'd been staging a protest. Ethelbert was in a terrible state, and stinking to high heaven. Wilhelmina got a smack and was sent straight to bed after taking one sniff at him and declaring with disgust, 'You've pissed yourself!'

Tom screwed up his face as though tempted to make a similar comment, but, having seen his sister packed off to bed, he controlled himself. 'Phew! You don't half pong!' he shouted as he fled into the scullery to join Lucky under the table.

70

I said nothing. But I suddenly remembered I had a job to do in the salon.

'I ain't never seen a room cleared so bloody quick in all me life!' said Ethelbert, while Maggie lovingly set about peeling off his sodden trousers. 'Just wait till I claps eyes on them filthy dogs agin! . . . I'll lerrem 'ave both bloody barrels up the arse, I will! Fancy cocking yer leg up a poor 'elpless feller when 'e's tied to the railings!' (I bet the Council wallahs put the dogs up to it!)

'It's a disgrace,' agreed Maggie, holding the offending trousers at arm's length while she carried them outside. '*Four* of them, there were . . . roving about in a pack and relieving themselves on anything that was tied down. It's disgraceful! I shall have words to say to the authorities on Monday morning, you see if I don't!'

When the last intruder went from next door, Maggie broke in through the back-room window. She and Ethelbert climbed inside and refused to come out. 'Well, I'm buggered!' roared Sonya. 'Casey's Court's gorra couple o' geriatric squatters!' (It's all right for her. *She* doesn't have to keep them supplied with tea and Steradent.)

At nine P.M. the whole street was out when an ambulance tore down the road with its siren going and its light flashing. Poor old Fred Twistle was carted off to the infirmary. 'It's all the excitement,' declared the woman from the tripe shop.

'Naw, it ain't,' rejoined Sonya. 'He's like the rest of us . . . worried sick that he might lose his home. What! Fred and Bertha Twistle 'ave been in that there 'ouse sin' they were wed fifty year ago. No wonder 'is 'eart gave out . . . poor old sod.'

Bertha's gone a bit funny too. 'Yer can sod off, all of yer!' she yelled, shaking her fat little fist from the doorstep. ''E'll be back! My Fred'll be back. *Then* we'll see

71

whether the Council can shift us!' When I went to talk quietly to her, she brandished a broom at me. 'I told yous to sod off, and that's just what I meant!'

The gentle Larkin made an effort. 'You're distraught, Bertha,' she coaxed. 'We're all your friends. Will you let *me* come in and sit with you a while?' When all she got for her trouble was the curt instruction to 'Keep away from me, you bloody wind-bag!' the poor little thing ran in sobbing.

'Oh, bloody Nora! We'll none of us get any sleep now . . . she'll be blowing off till *all* hours!' wailed Sonya.

After Bertha had gone in and banged the door, I telephoned the police station. 'What have you been up to now?' demanded my favourite helmet. His attitude softened once I explained how Bertha's husband had suffered a heart attack and she'd locked herself in.

'It's most unlike the old dear,' I said. 'She ought to have help.' He actually thanked me and promised to get a social worker out. (They do say, Lord, that you send these things to try us. Well, congratulations, because I'm well and truly knackered. Goodnight.)

Sunday, January 29th

I couldn't eat a thing today, although when I got the dinner plates back through the window of next door I was pleased to see that Maggie and Ethelbert's appetites were healthy enough. I'm worried sick, though, because I can't help feeling that the Council will go berserk when they find they've got squatters in No. 3. And what if the house is really in danger of collapsing? Oh, it doesn't bear thinking about. When I expressed the same argument to Maggie, she made Tom fetch her tin hat, and an old enamel bowl for Ethelbert. 'You don't frighten *us*,' she said. 'We'll *never* flinch in the face of danger . . . will we, chichicoo?"

'*Never!*' Ethelbert replied, looking a real warrior with his popgun pointed at the door and the enamel bowl on his head.

Sonya peeped through the window to have a look at them. I had hoped she might try and talk some sense into them, but all she did was laugh out loud. 'Yer both daft as arse'oles,' she said. 'Serves yer right if they lock yer up in the asylum.' Then she gave me a hand to push some home comforts through the window . . . a mattress, blankets, toiletries and a kerosene lamp. I could see Maggie getting agitated and trying to attract my attention.

'What is it, Maggie?' I asked, assuring her that I had put a roll of toilet paper in the cardboard box.

'No, it isn't that, Jessy,' she whispered, yanking me to the far corner of the window. 'I want that Oxo tin out of the right hand drawer in my dressing table.'

Sonya heard her. 'I'll get it,' she offered, rushing away. 'Don't fret yersel, darlin'.'

It was most unfortunate that Sonya was the one to fetch the Oxo tin, because, being naturally nosy, she couldn't resist having a peek inside. 'Well, I'm buggered!' she cried, handing the tin to the nervously waiting Maggie. 'I wouldn't have thought you two needed French letters! At your age all yer necessaries must a' shrivelled up long since.'

Maggie was horrified. 'Sonya Pitts,' she said in her most dignified manner, 'I'm astonished that you had the nerve to search my private box. It's inconceivable!'

''Tain't,' retorted the unabashed Sonya, 'it's *you two* that's "inconceivable". I'd throw them things away if I

73

were you. Be daring and dangerous in yer old age, why don't yer?'

At which point Maggie slammed down the window. 'I'll call you if I need you, Jessy,' she shouted. I could tell she was upset when I heard her inform Ethelbert, 'From now on you'll put your own condoms on . . . and to hell with your bad back!' (Poor old sod. He couldn't fathom out what he'd done wrong.)

Bertha Twistle wouldn't let the social worker in. I've tried talking to her through the letter box, but she won't answer. I told her I'd phoned the infirmary and found out that Fred was on the mend. But I don't know whether she felt pleased or not at the news, because it's common knowledge that the pair of them have lately been fighting like cat and dog. At one point, the woman from the tripe shop heard Bertha say she'd be glad 'when the old fool's dead and gone . . . then I can stuff myself with pigeon pie and me and my cats can live in peace.'

Personally, I'm convinced that's half their problem. I've said it before and I'll say it again . . . it's a mistake to harbour cats and pigeons under the same roof. Anyway, Sonya, little Larkin and I are going to take it in turns to leave a small food parcel on Bertha's front doorstep. We can't let the poor dear starve to death. What with her barricading herself in, and those two old desperadoes next door, I feel harassed to death. (And they say it's the *young* ones who cause the bother in this world! It only goes to show that they haven't met the old relics from Casey's Court!)

Monday, January 30th

I had another letter this morning from that persistent
solicitor. When I told Maggie, she was of the same
opinion as Sonya. 'Offered you another five thousand
pounds!' exploded Sonya. 'That proves it, then. It *is*
Barny Singleton, because altogether 'e's offering *more*
than the place is worth. The sod just wants you out o' the
'airdressing business . . . wants to rid 'isself o' the
competition!'

Maggie was furious. But Ethelbert was puzzled.
'There's some'at fishy going on 'ere, Jessy,' he said
quietly. 'To be honest, I don't think it *is* Barny . . . 'cause
I reckon 'e'd ask yer straight out, like 'e's done afore.
Why go through a solicitor? It don't mek sense to me.'

'Well, it wouldn't, would it?' said Maggie, lovingly
putting a tender arm round his shoulder. 'You haven't got
a devious thought in your head, bless your old heart.'
Whereupon she began sucking his ear.

'Be buggered!' yelled Sonya. 'They don't come no more
devious than that old sod. Tek no notice of 'im . . . 'cause
'e's just sticking up for a fellow mate. All men together
an' get the upper 'and o'er the women folk. They're all
the bloody same, is fellers.'

The row raged on, until I caught a glimpse of Barny
drawing up at his house around noon. So, clutching the
letter, I went over and thrust it under his nose. 'Explain
that,' I asked him, afterwards waiting impatiently while
he carefully read it. I must admit, he looked innocent
enough, because I watched his expression like a hawk as
his eyes scanned the letter.

When he handed it back, saying, '*I* can't explain it,
Jessy sweetheart . . . what makes you think I can?' he

looked positively wounded. I pressed him further, accusing him of being the only one to gain from my selling the business, but he told me I was barking up the wrong tree. 'How can I even think of marrying a woman who has such little trust in me?' he demanded, before slamming off into his house. I felt a real twit . . . especially when I turned round to see a bevy of faces gawping at me from the salon window, Ethelbert and Maggie, both toothless, peering from the empty house next door, and net curtains curiously moving all along Casey's Court.

Of a sudden, the salon window was flung open and Sonya's blonde head appeared through it. ''E's a liar!' she yelled at the top of her voice. 'A bloody liar. Gerrin there after 'im, go on! Mek the traitor confess!'

My one thought being to shut her up before the whole of Casey's Court came out on the street, I dashed back across the road, rushed indoors and grabbed my coat. 'I don't think it *is* him,' I told her, 'but I'll find out, because I'm going straight down to the solicitor's.'

'It *is* Barny Singleton, an' if yer weren't so bloody daft ye'd see it,' accused Sonya. 'Yer let the bugger blind yer wi' 'is empty talk of marrying yer . . . what! That feller ain't got no more intention o' marrying yer than your Maggie 'as need of them bloody condoms.' (There are times when I could cheerfully wring Sonya's neck!)

I got next to nothing from the solicitor. 'We're like doctors, in the sense that we are bound to respect a client's confidence,' he said sweetly. When I threatened to sue him, he showed me the door. 'Good day, Mrs Jolly . . . go to another solicitor if you feel the need. But you'll only be told the same. My client has expressed the wish that his identity be concealed. All I can tell you is that he is most keen to purchase your property lock, stock and barrel . . . and is prepared to be most generous in the event, as you can see from the figure disclosed.'

On the way home, I mulled over his words, and was bound to consider whether it really *was* Barny who was after my home and business. It *was* a man . . . the solicitor had given that much away at least. When I got back, I sat down and wrote a long letter to him stating most categorically that No. 2 Casey's Court was *not* for sale, and never would be. Not at *any* price, and would he please convey that once and for all to his client. I also informed him that any further correspondence on the subject would be burned. As far as I was concerned, that was an end to the matter.

'That's telled the bugger,' laughed Sonya, who insisted on looking over my shoulder as I wrote. 'When Barny Singleton's told that, 'e'll get the right message, I'm sure.'

I've lain awake for hours, wondering whether Sonya's right. *Is* it Barny? Could he really be so devious? I'm undecided. But that letter should do the trick. (I hope so, because there's something badly upsetting about knowing that somebody, who won't reveal his identity, is hellbent on acquiring the very roof over your head . . . even if he is paying handsomely for it.)

Tuesday, January 31st

At midnight, I heard banging and shouting outside. When I peeked through the back window, it was to see Maggie and Ethelbert standing in the yard. 'Open up and let us come in out of the cold,' she yelled. It took a long time for her to admit that the scampering mice had 'put the fear of God up me!' (And I thought she was afraid of nothing.)

I had a gorgeous bouquet of flowers from Barny this morning. The card said, 'I hate being in your bad books. Especially when I'm innocent. Love you.' It was a beautiful gesture. 'And I love you too, Barny,' I murmured, as I tenderly put the flowers in a vase, 'that's the trouble.'

Sonya knew who they were from the minute she saw them. 'Ever 'eard o' the Trojan 'orse?' she asked sarcastically, throwing on her smock and marching into the salon. She was in a funny mood all morning. At one point I thought she'd drowned the woman from the tripe shop, when she thrust the poor dear's head into the bowl and turned the hand-shower on full blast at her. If it hadn't been for the fact that I happened to see two arms frantically thrashing about and a pair of short dumpy legs straight up in the air, she would have been a gonner for sure. 'Yer a silly arse,' Sonya told her after I'd saved the terrified creature. 'Why didn't yer *tell* me yer 'ad a mouth full o' water?' (It was some ten minutes before the poor woman could utter a word.)

Wednesday, February 1st

Maggie spent all morning writing letters. I thought it best not to antagonize her, so I left her to get on with it. I did stop her for a cup of coffee in the afternoon, during a lull in the salon. 'Have a look at this,' I said, passing her a letter which had been hand-delivered about four P.M. It was from the Council, and according to Sonya's network of spies every householder in Casey's Court had received one.

'The buggers claim that the 'ouses are fallin' down,' she told Maggie while she was reading, 'an' if yer ask me, it's just an excuse ter demolish the lot.'

Before passions were roused any further, I intervened to explain that the letter intimated nothing of the kind, and that in *my* opinion we should all examine the situation in a calm and controlled manner instead of letting our imaginations, and our tempers, run away with us. I then rang the Council office and told them in no uncertain terms that if they *were* trying to pull the wool over our eyes 'you'll have a bloody riot on your hands!' (I'm ashamed to say I lost control and it all ended in a blazing row.)

In no time at all, Marny Tupp from the Barge Inn had delivered a message of his own, urging everyone to attend an important meeting in the back room of his residence at eight P.M. Everybody was there, and there was a deal of heated exchange. I had to tell them about my discovery that the wall joining us and next door *was* actually sinking. The information went down like a bombshell, and for a moment they were all speechless. Then, lo and behold, there was unleashed a torrent of 'confessions' about 'sinking floors', 'cracks from floor to ceiling' and roofs 'split open to the stars'.

'It's right,' said Big Betty. 'I put a joint o' beef in the oven a' Sunday . . . and I'm buggered if the weight of it didn't send me cooker legs right through the floor. It didn't spoil the *joint*, mind yer. But my Jack were that mad, 'cause his Yorkshire pud were flat as a pancake.'

When the meeting had drawn to a noisy close, it was reluctantly agreed that the Council was right in claiming that the houses were in a dangerous condition. It was also agreed that they would be demolished 'only over our dead bodies!' Marny Tupp, having appointed himself spokesman, will write to anyone and everyone who might support our cause, for a permanent solution to the problem. It was also agreed that if any Council snooper was seen loitering about Casey's Court 'yer all ter set yer dogs on 'em!' (Lucky won't think much of that. He prefers chasing Fred Twistle's pigeons.)

After the meeting, I phoned the infirmary, then I went along to Bertha Twistle's house. 'Your Fred's holding his own, Bertha,' I shouted through the letter box, hoping she'd let me in.

'Piss orf!' came the sharp response. 'I don't give a bugger whose he's holding.' No amount of cajoling or reasoning would persuade her to open the door and let me in.

'All right then . . . I'll leave your box of groceries on the doorstep tomorrow,' I told her.

As I walked away, I could hear her voice at the letter box. 'Fred Twistle's allus thought more of his bloody pigeons than ever he has o' me! So let the bugger hold his own – or anybody else's – and see if *I* care! And don't ask *me* ter bury the divil . . . 'cause I'd as soon throw 'im down the tip!'

'Poor ol' cow,' said Sonya when I told her. 'She's right, though . . . ol' Fred did everything but mek love ter them pigeons. No wonder ol' Bertha's gone orf 'im. I'm surprised she ain't wrung them pigeons' necks afore now, an' all.'

'No, she wouldn't do that, would she? After all, it's not *their* fault.' I was horrified at the thought. But to Sonya it was just another source of amusement.

'I bet ol' Bertha's 'ad pigeon pie every day since Fred were tekken away,' she laughed. (I must find out if they're safe and being fed.)

I sent our Tom round to ask Bertha whether she'd like him to come and clean out the pigeon loft. He came rushing back all wet and angry. 'That Bertha Twistle should be put away,' he said indignantly. 'I shouted through the letter box and told her what you said. She threw a bowl o' soapy water at me, and told me to sod off, else she'd have me eyes out.' It took me ages to calm the poor little thing. He was convinced *I'd* done it on purpose. 'You *want* Bertha Twistle to blind me,' he cried, 'then I can't watch Maggie and Ethelbert playing at mums and dads.' (I'm at the end of my tether.)

The kind-faced man came to the salon today, and asked for me specifically to cut his hair. 'I'm sure I lost half an inch off both my ears when Sonya did it before,' he laughed. (He may not be the world's best looker, but he does have a lovely smile. And those navy-blue eyes are really attractive . . . kind of filled with mischief.)

It was only after he'd gone that I realized just how much of my life story he'd managed to draw out of me. I confided things in him that I'd never told any other living soul: that I was never really happy with Vernon Jolly, and that in all the years we were married, before he passed on, I had never once suspected what a womanizing cheat he was. I told him I considered myself a failure as a mother, and how Tom and Wilhelmina brought me to screaming pitch just by opening their mouths. Yet there were other times . . . rare but wonderful . . . when I would die for them. I even confided my love for Barny . . . and the suspicions which had lately developed.

'Cor, bloody Nora!' exclaimed Sonya, when he'd gone. 'Why didn't yer tell 'im what colour yer knickers were?' She'd heard it all. Funny thing, though. In spite of my pouring out my heart to him, he had told me absolutely *nothing* about himself. Sonya had pulled a fast one, though. 'While 'e were so intent on listening ter you, I snuck out an' took a peep in 'is van,' she explained. 'All 'is vehicle documents were in the glove compartment. 'Is name's Craig Forester, an' 'e comes from Accrington. There's all sort o' tools in the back of 'is van . . . building tools . . . chisels, paint and the like. Funny, ain't it, gal? Why does a feller come all the way from Accrington ter Oswaldtwistle, just ter gerris 'air cut?'

'Well, he's probably doing a job round these parts, and it's too late for him to get to the barber's after a day's work.' I could see that Sonya still wasn't convinced, and nor was I. For one thing, Craig Forester was always smartly dressed when he came here, so he couldn't be on a building job. For another, he was too nosy by half.

'Lovely feller, though, ain't 'e?' Sonya smiled, seeing me deep in thought. And she was right. He *was* a 'lovely feller', and I liked him more than I cared to admit.

We had *another* unexpected visitor to the shop. But he only wanted to see whether Maggie and Ethelbert would be coming to his warehouse 'fer them few household odds an' ends'. It was Tipples, the rag-a-bone man. 'Tell 'im ter bugger off!' muttered Sonya, when she saw his horse and cart pull up. I was amazed when she quickly retreated into the back parlour, her face all shades of crimson. It's the very first time I've ever seen her blush.

'What did you run off like that for?' I asked her when he'd gone. 'He only wanted to know whether Maggie and Ethelbert were moving in next door.'

'Tipples is like *all* bloody men,' she retorted, still agitated, 'too nosy by 'alf.' It suddenly struck me that Sonya was still in love with Tipples. Bless her heart. I wonder if there's a way to get the pair of them together again? Ah, but, if I remember rightly, Ethelbert said Tipples had never forgiven her for rejecting him. Still and all, I'm sure I'll think of something.

Friday, February 3rd

Smelly Kelly's got himself a new woman. 'Right tarty piece she is!' Sonya said.

'Aye well . . . so are you,' retorted Maggie, 'and he had a fling with you once. So he must be partial to "tarty pieces".' (Maggie can be really crabby when she wants.)

Later, I took her to task over it. 'Don't be so cruel, Maggie,' I chided, 'you're getting nasty in your old age.' She was really upset, and went upstairs for a sulking fit.

'See what you've done!' accused Ethelbert. 'I'll not get my treats tonight.' (Well! Neither will I.)

Barny's cried off from our date tomorrow night. He made some feeble excuse about 'not feeling too well', but he looked all right to me. Sonya's convinced he's arranged to see the dark buxom beauty instead. 'We'll set a trap for 'em, gal,' she said, 'catch the dirty dog red'anded.' She even recruited Maggie's help (nice to see them friends again). Ethelbert flatly refused.

'I think it's a rotten thing to do,' he said. 'Why, they might be up ter all manner o' things when yer burst in on 'em. Naw . . . count me out, 'cause I'll not play a filthy trick like that on a poor feller.' (He should have kept his mouth shut, because now Maggie's stopped his 'treats' for a week.)

I'm not too keen on the idea either, to be honest. But I *have* to know whether Barny really is two-timing me. There was one thing I *did* put my foot down about, though. 'I'm not having you bursting in on them, so we'll

83

have to catch her when she's leaving . . . then march her back inside to confront him with the truth.' I really couldn't face storming in, only to see her enjoying what he's never given me.

Saturday, February 4th

I felt too preoccupied to think straight today, and I woke up with a splitting headache. (I suppose it could have something to do with that little swine Tom beating me over the head with his rubber duck.)

The salon was full to bursting from the minute we opened to five o'clock when we closed. 'I tell yer what, gal,' said Sonya, buckling at the knees and gasping for a cuppa, 'if it goes on like this ye'll 'ave ter gerranother assistant. I can't be going 'ome knackered, y'know . . . there's me reg'lar fellers ter think of, an' they're very demanding. Especially Wally Entwistle.' I knew she was dying to tell me why Wally Entwistle was 'especially demanding', so I quickly changed the subject, thinking I might draw her into confiding other matters close to her heart.

'That Tipples is a nice chap, don't you think?' I asked in a matter of fact way. 'Beneath all those rags and tatters, he's a bit of a rough diamond . . . and he has the merriest green eyes.'

But Sonya wasn't biting. Instead, she was pretending to check the stock. 'Ain't never noticed,' she snorted. 'Anyway . . . we're running short on "Kiss'n'curl" an' there's only two extra-long condoms left.'

Whereupon Maggie, being in the vicinity, dashed forward smartly and snapped them up. '*I'll* have these,' she

84

muttered, dropping the money in the till and scurrying away.

'Hmph!' laughed Sonya. 'Some folks 'ave bigger dreams than others!' Whatever would she say if she knew about *my* dreams? Funny, though, how they swing between Barny and Craig Forester. Two lovely fellows, and neither of them mine. (I'm getting desperate.)

About quarter to five, when Maggie and Ethelbert had taken the brats off to the pictures and Sonya was helping me clear up the salon, there came an almighty crash from the back parlour. 'Hell's bells,' exclaimed Sonya, grabbing a particularly spiky hair brush. 'That's either yer old ghostie started up agin, else ye've got burglars!'

'Shut the door, Sonya,' I whispered, backing away like the coward I am. 'We'll barricade ourselves in here till the constable arrives.' I felt instinctively that it wasn't our 'ghostie' (old Pops, the former owner of the barber-shop) because he'd been content and quiet since we reopened. 'There's somebody in there . . . I *know* it's a burglar.' It suddenly struck me that it could be Lucky, and Sonya seemed to agree.

'O' course, yer silly arse,' she laughed, beginning to make her way to the parlour. (I wish I was as brave as she is.) 'What yer doing, yer mangy bugger?' (For a minute there I was convinced she was talking to me, as I cowered in the salon waiting for the all-clear.)

'Well, I'm buggered! 'Ere, Jessy . . . come an' look at this,' shouted Sonya. When I got to the parlour, I couldn't believe my eyes. Half the floorboards were up. 'I thought yer said the floor were sinking?' said Sonya. 'This bugger looks like it's raised from the dead!'

Neither of us could make head nor tail of it. The boards looked as if they'd been actually taken up one by one . . . very carefully. And there were little piles of dirt and muck everywhere. 'It looks as if somebody's been searching about underneath the floor,' I said. I couldn't think what *else* might have caused such an upheaval.

'Either that or ye've got some bloody big rats!' remarked Sonya. 'But who the 'ell would want ter tek up the floor . . . an' what did they expect ter find underneath?' Usually Sonya had all the answers, but she was as perplexed as I was. We both agreed that Lucky couldn't have done it. So it was one of three things: old Pops was haunting us again; there had been an intruder; or the houses were dangerously unsafe and somehow part of the floor had lifted.

Later, when Sonya and I had replaced the area of floor, and Maggie was back, I put the three possibilities to her. She was in no doubt. 'There's been an intruder, Jessy . . . the other two don't make sense.'

Ethelbert, however, was equally adamant. 'Don't talk out the back o' yer 'ead, woman. What the 'ell would an intruder want from underneath the bloody floorboards?' He pointed out that my handbag was untouched, and so was the cash tin, which was easily accessible in the sideboard drawer. 'An' old Pops only 'aunted this place when 'e thought the authorities wouldn't let Jessy open the barber's agin! Naw . . . I'm tellin' yer it's these old 'ouses. The foundations is in a state of upheaval, *that's* what's done it.'

Tom and Wilhelmina gave their opinion (which, incidentally, I never asked for). 'We think it was Lucky,' they piped up in unison. 'Yeah . . . *you* don't know how strong he is,' said Tom smugly. '*We* know, though,' chimed in Smarty-pants, 'but we're not telling, are we, Tom?' (I hate kids!)

It was unanimously decided that we wouldn't report the incident, because the Council might use it to support their argument that the houses should be demolished. Afterwards, Tom and Wilhelmina took Lucky down the rec as a reward for his 'clever trick', while Maggie and Ethelbert went off collecting signatures in their commendable pursuit of the house next door. And Sonya hurried away to 'get ready for Wally Entwistle'. I was hoping she'd forgotten the business of trapping Barny and his buxom beauty. But such hopes were dashed when she turned at the door to remind me. 'I'll be back about nine o'clock, when ye've put the kids to bed. Then we can all tek it in turns ter watch that snake in the grass across the road!'

True to her word, Sonya came back at quarter past nine, breathless and dishevelled. 'Gawd!' she gasped, falling in the door. ''E's a little divil is that Wally Entwistle. The bugger's fair worn me out.' (She looked as if she'd been ten rounds with Mike Tyson.)

After much discussion, and an argument from me that I didn't care for the idea of snooping on Barny (for which I was promptly told by Sonya to 'shut yer gob, yer soft cow') we took up our positions . . . Sonya and I at the salon window and Maggie upstairs with Ethelbert. 'An' none o' yer bloody shenanigans, you two!' warned Sonya. 'Ye'll 'ave ter control yerselves, 'cause if I 'ear so much as that bed creak I'll be up them stairs like a bat out of 'ell.' Maggie's sulking now. She was particularly peeved when Sonya made a sneering remark about the contents of Maggie's pocket. 'Condoms . . . at *your* age! Extra-bloody-long!' she laughed (quite unnecessarily, I thought). 'If yer ask me, the only use you two could 'ave fer them is to sling the buggers together for an 'ammock!'

Ethelbert told her in no uncertain terms to 'Wash yer mouth out, my gal . . . else ye'll feel the weight o' me foot up yer arse!' (It's a unique experience, seeing Sonya speechless. It didn't last, though.)

'Garn, yer little git!' she said, with a twinkle in her eye. 'I've swallered bigger worms than you fer breakfast.' (On reflection I don't think Tiffany *would* fit in here.)

For two long uncomfortable hours, there was no sign of movement from Barny's house, except for the upstairs light flashing on and off every few minutes. 'The buggers are up there at it,' Sonya said, digging me hard in the ribs. 'I expect she 'as ter keep switching on the light so's she can find 'is periwinkle.'

I got really angry with her at one point. 'You've no call to go saying such things,' I told her. 'I'm convinced Barny's as well endowed as most men . . . if not *better*.' She didn't say anything but she gave me one of those infuriating old-fashioned looks.

By eleven o'clock, I began to wonder what I was doing hiding there in the dark, with Sonya telling me one lewd joke after another, and the sound of Maggie and Ethelbert's snoring echoing round the house. 'Cor, bugger me, gal,' Sonya said, 'the silly sods 'ave fell asleep on the job.' She was all for going up there and giving them what for, but I was having none of it.

'Leave them be,' I said firmly. 'They're not so young as they used to be. Besides, I think we're all wasting our time, because there's only *Barny* in that house, and he's doing nothing more sinister than preparing to go to bed.'

No sooner had I finished speaking than the light went out in Barny's bedroom. In a minute, the hallway light was on, and Sonya was beside herself with excitement. 'Quick, gal,' she cried, going for the door, 'we'll catch 'er as she comes out!' Without further ado, she was away up the passage, with me beside her. At the door she composed herself and peered out through the letter box. 'Give 'er time to gerrout on the pavement . . . then we'll sprint across the road an' grab the bugger. She won't know what's 'it 'er . . . an' neither will that two-timing Barny when we confront 'im with 'er, eh? Oh, that'll give 'im a shock, I'll be bound!' (I wish I'd chickened out earlier. Now it was too late.)

All my guilty feelings disappeared when Barny's front door opened and out came a tall, striking figure whose silhouette, outlined by the hall light, would make strong men weep. Her dark hair cascaded over her shoulders and when she began walking away, with the most disgustingly delicious hip-wiggle, I felt desperately inferior.

'Must we go through with it?' I whispered into the darkness.

'Too bloody true we must!' declared Sonya, legging it across the road with me in tow. 'Hey, you! Just 'ang on a minute, me beauty,' she yelled at the disappearing figure, 'me an' my mate 'ere want a word!'

The buxom beauty took one frightened look at the pair of us bearing down on her and, with a cry of alarm, kicked off her shoes and ran as if the very devil was after her. (Having witnessed Sonya in full charge, I can't say I blamed her.) 'You keep away. Keep away!' came a terrified cry. I could tell she was petrified, because her voice was all hoarse and peculiar. But there was no turning back now. Sonya was right. She'd been right all along, and now I wanted to know the truth. Barny wouldn't level with me, so there was nothing else for it but to catch the woman who'd just come out of his house. The thought of him two-timing me was really hurtful, but I had to know for sure.

She led us a merry dance . . . out of Casey's Court, down Rosamund Street and into Victoria's Alley. (Boy, could she run!) 'Gawd love us!' panted Sonya. 'She's been training for the marathon.' At the bottom of Pump Street, Sonya grabbed hold of her. 'Gotcha, yer bugger!' she yelled, clinging on for dear life as the desperate woman fought like a wildcat. 'Ye've been 'aving it off wi' me mate's feller, ain't yer, eh?'

As for me, after all that running I couldn't breathe. My chest felt as if it was encased in steel straps, and my legs were buckling under me. 'Go easy, Sonya,' I pleaded between painful gasps. 'All I want is the truth . . . not a lynching.'

Of a sudden, Sonya let out a shriek as the buxom beauty thumped her one and tore away up the road. By the time Sonya had recovered from the blow, our only evidence was long gone. 'Sod an' bugger it,' cried Sonya, 'we've lost 'er now.' (Funny thing – I felt quite relieved.)

'Yer know, gal,' Sonya said quietly as we made our way back to Casey's Court, 'there's some'at strange about that woman . . . but for the life o' me I can't put me finger on it.' She looked a real sketch, hobbling on one heel, the other having snapped off in a grating. With her hair all asunder after her desperate tussle, she looked like the wild man from Borneo. 'No, Jessy,' she went on, 'I've got this feeling that I've seen 'er afore somewhere. By! I'll tell yer what, though, gal . . . she's strong as a lion, an' built like a tank.' All the way home she kept muttering, 'Strange . . . right bloody strange.' But she wouldn't be drawn any further on the subject, except to blurt out when we got to our front door, 'I can't mek 'ead nor tail on it, Jessy gal. 'Ere . . . look at this.' She dug into her coat pocket to produce something stiff and lumpy.

'Whatever is it?' I asked, having a feel.

'Dunno fer sure, gal,' she replied in an odd voice, 'but it came off in me 'and when I wrestled wi' 'er. If yer ask me, it's 'er tit!'

'Don't be so daft, Sonya,' I said, shocked. 'Get off

90

home and go to bed. We're all tired. How can her . . . thingie . . . come off in your hand?'

''Tain't no use trying ter humour me, gal,' she snorted. 'This 'ere's a tit, I'm telling yer . . . one o' them cheap an' nasty falsies. I do know what I'm talkin' about, y'know! I've seen it all afore!' With that, she rammed the offending article back in her pocket and strode away. 'I'll get ter the bottom of it,' she called out behind her, 'you see if I don't. What's more, if I see 'er on the street, I'll know the tart, because I managed ter fetch 'er a real beauty in the eye. Oh, I'm tellin' yer, Jessy . . . she'll be sportin' a right shiner tomorrer.'

Here it is, nearly two A.M., and I still can't settle. It's been a terrible evening . . . what with catching that woman coming out of Barny's house, and Sonya's ridiculous claim that she was wearing falsies. It doesn't make sense. What would Barny want with a woman who wears falsies? What's more, she was quite big and muscular close up. I mean, you'd only to see how she went down that road like a trained athlete. Oh, but I mustn't kid myself, because she really is very attractive. She's got such a shapely figure, and that thick black hair is just the kind that men like to run their fingers through. There's no two ways about it, Barny's 'bit on the side' is tall, statuesque and full of life. While I'm short, a little on the dumpy side and too exhausted by life to stand up and fight it.

I'll tell Barny tomorrow that I won't hold him against his will. He can stop smuggling her in and out, because I won't stand in their way any more. (Dear Lord, I know I'm a coward. But you made me that way, so it's *your* fault!)

Three times I went and knocked on Barny's door today. But he wouldn't let me in. 'Go away,' he yelled at me from the top of the stairs when I peered through the letter box. 'I'm not well enough to receive visitors.' When I suggested that I could look after him, he made it quite clear that he wanted to be left alone. So I left him to it. There'll be time enough later to have a serious talk about our relationship.

Sonya wasn't at all surprised that he was feeling under the weather. 'I'm feeling a bit frayed at the edges meself, after that bundle with 'is bit o' fluff . . . or should I say that couple o' rounds with 'is all-in wrestler? I never would 'a reckoned Barny Singleton to be the type as went for masculine women, an' bits that come off in yer 'and.' (I've got the most diabolical headache now.)

This afternoon, Sonya very kindly minded the kids while Maggie, Ethelbert and I went to visit old Fred Twistle. When I popped down the street to ask Bertha whether she wanted to come, or to send a message, she became very hostile and rude, giving me a real mouthful through the window. It really isn't like her at all. There was no way I could bring myself to deliver her message to Fred. It could bring on another heart attack if I were to tell him that Bertha sent the same regards as she felt for his precious pigeons, 'and I've just finished *stuffing* the last o' *them*, tell him!' At least she's started coming out and going to the shops. But she's so sharp and surly, everybody steers well clear of her. I keep trying to be friendly. But when you're constantly being told to 'piss off, yer interfering bugger' it rather takes the heart out of you. All the same, I can't help but feel sorry for her. I'm sure there's something psychological at the bottom of it all, because, in spite of all the rows she and Fred had over her cats and his pigeons, they really were very fond of each other.

I had intended taking Sonya and the kids along to the infirmary with us, because I thought she might cheer old Fred up. I changed my mind, though, when she made her intentions clear. 'I shan't beat about the bush, Jessy gal. The poor sod 'as every right ter know that she won't lerrim in when he's discharged. They'll 'ave ter purrim in the knacker's yard, an' 'e might as well know now as later.'

Old Fred looked no end better, bless him. 'You tell my old gal as I understand why she ain't come ter see me. It's all right, tell 'er, 'cause I'll be back 'ome in no time at all.' Then he went shy and blushed crimson. 'I miss the ol' cow,' he murmured. 'Yer can tell 'er that, if yer like.' He also gave me a list of dos and don'ts with regard to his pigeons. 'Them's priceless ter me,' he said, 'they're me pals, every one of 'em.' (Oh dear!)

I went straight down to Bertha's when I got back, but she wouldn't let me in. 'Say what you've come to say, then be off!' she yelled at me from the window. When I passed on Fred's message she looked choked up with emotion. For a minute I thought she was going to let me in, because she disappeared from the window and after a while the front door was inched open. 'He sent you this as well, Bertha,' I said, poking the list of dos and don'ts through the gap. 'It's about his pigeons, I think.'

'Oh, it's about his bloody *pigeons*, is it?' came the angry voice. 'So you *didn't* give him the message about me having stuffed the last of 'em, eh? Well now, you can tek this 'ere list an' tell him to stuff it in the same way . . . up his arse as far as he can!' With that, she flung the paper

93

on to the pavement and slammed the door. (Where will it all end, I ask myself.)

Monday, February 6th

There was no sign of life over at Barny's when I opened my curtains this morning, so I quickly dressed and rattled his front door. But his bedroom curtains remained shut and I couldn't get any reply. 'Leave 'im alone,' advised Sonya in her usual heartless way. 'If 'e's feeling rotten, then 'e's got nobody else ter blame but 'imself. I expect that tart's rung 'im up an' warned 'im ter lay low fer a while. No doubt she's told 'im we nearly purran end to their nasty little games, an' the coward's staying put till it's safe ter come out.'

I did manage to get him on the phone when Sonya was busy trimming Smelly Kelly's beard, but he wasn't very sociable. 'I've just got a bit of a tummy upset,' he told me. 'A bit of peace and quiet and I'll be right as ninepence in no time.'

'Tummy upset be buggered,' scoffed Sonya when we were having our tea break. I told her that I couldn't help but feel worried about him, and that I thought a dose of Andrews might shift his problem. She was not a bit sympathetic. 'As far as I'm concerned, the only thing to shift 'is problem is a swift kick up the cobblers! That Barny Singleton's giving you the run-around, Jessy, an' well yer know it,' she roared. Maggie endorsed her opinion, but Ethelbert wouldn't be drawn in.

'Barny's young,' he said, 'an' all young men are entitled to sow a few wild oats.'

'Oh, yes? And *you'd* know all about that, wouldn't you, Ethelbert Pitts?' said Maggie, flashing him a piercing

94

look. 'Because you've spread a few wild oats in your time . . . not the least of which is the woman from the tripe shop.' It looked like the beginnings of a row, until Ethelbert squeezed her knee and slapped his mouth over the back of her hand.

'None wilder than you, me darlin' . . . an' none so lovely,' he cooed.

'Cor, bloody Nora!' declared Sonya. 'Don't it mek yer sick, eh?' (I was just thinking the same thing, as I watched her fishing about with her fingers for the biscuit she'd lost in her tea cup.)

Tom's got a girlfriend. 'Her name's Nelly,' he told Wilhelmina proudly, grinning broadly from ear to ear.

'I *know* who she is,' replied Miss Clever-clogs. '*We* call her Nelly with the wooden belly.' (Obnoxious child!)

There was another meeting at the town hall today. It seems they're split fifty fifty over whether to demolish Casey's Court or modernize all the houses while keeping the character intact. Apparently, because there was no majority vote, it has to be decided by a special commission. It's all very frustrating. On top of everything else, if Maggie and Ethelbert don't soon get their own house, I think I'll go mad. They're all right on their own, but when they're together they've got no shame. (It's thanks to them I've started getting hot flushes.)

Lucky wandered in with a Staffordshire terrier today. It was really fierce. When Maggie chased it out with a broom, it bit the head clean off. Lucky was so proud. The two of them went off up the road arm in arm. (I must stop treating him to fish heads. He's getting above himself.)

Pancake day! Maggie's been stuffing them down us till we're positively bloated. 'You eat them all up,' she ordered Tom when he complained of tummy pains. 'I haven't spent hours over that stove to see them go to waste.' I wouldn't mind, but they're so stodgy each one weighs a ton. Wilhelmina slyly fed hers to poor Lucky. He's been waddling around with a look of pure martyrdom on his little face. 'What's to do wi' that dog?' asked Maggie. 'He looks constipated.'

'What's that?' Tom wanted to know. When Miss Clever-clogs explained, he pointed out that it wasn't true, because 'I saw him plop all over Bertha Twistle's front doorstep, and she chased him down the road with her long mop.'

I was reminded that old Fred was due home next week, so I made the wry comment to Maggie, 'I hope she doesn't do the same to him.'

'Oh, no, she won't, Mam,' said Tom, ''cause *he* can use the lavvy, and poor Lucky can't.' (Who invented kids?)

Barny's still holed up. And rumour has it that Bertha Twistle's been in touch with the infirmary to tell them she's putting all of Fred's belongings on to the pavement. 'I think she's afeared he'll murder her when he finds out she's nobbled his feathered friends,' said Tipples. 'What's more, I think she's well out o' line. Old Fred thought the world o' them pigeons.' I was too taken with Tipples' appearance to join in the conversation between him and Ethelbert. For a rag-a-bone man, he certainly looked surprisingly well scrubbed. Although his knees were still jutting out of his trousers, and his pumps looked the worse for wear, he had on a new jumper and there was not a speck of dirt beneath his nails. His lovely even teeth were brilliant white as always, and his ginger beard was smartly trimmed and washed.

''E's after yer, Sonya gal,' teased Ethelbert as we watched Tipples climb on to his cart before clicking his faithful horse away down the road. Sonya appeared not to have heard him.

'Come away, you old troublemaker,' chided Maggie, dragging him into the back parlour.

From a distance, I regarded Sonya, who was still glued to the window, her brown eyes soulful as they followed the rag-a-bone cart out of sight. All day she mooned about, every now and then glancing towards the window as though she might suddenly see Tipples there. (Oh, the lucky soul whose love life runs smooth, eh?)

I had a letter from Tiffany this morning. 'I'm off on a cruise,' she said, 'it's doctor's orders, because my nerves are ragged.' (So are mine, but all I get is a bottle of aspirin.)

We were kept busy in the salon today. We had two quite unexpected customers . . . one being the woman who keeps the chip shop on Rosamund Street. She usually has her hair done at Barny's place in town, but 'apparently Mr Singleton's laid up at the minute, and I don't want no snotty-nosed kid doing *my* hair!' (Sonya couldn't resist making the remark that 'Mr Singleton was more likely laid *down* than up.' When the chip shop woman asked what she meant, Sonya told her, 'All our sins come 'ome ter roost.' The chip shop woman nodded her head, saying, 'Oh, I see.' But she looked totally confused.)

The other customer I didn't expect was that nice-looking fellow, Craig Forester. He actually asked me out to the pictures on Saturday. On impulse I said yes. But I've got a feeling I might live to regret it.

Wednesday, February 8th

We had to fetch Lucky from the dog compound at the police station. According to the dog-catcher who scooped him up in his net, Lucky was having an almighty row with a female Staffordshire terrier, who then ran off with a big brown poodle of the male sex and well endowed. It seems Lucky was devastated and tried to commit suicide by lying in front of the milk float. (He's been hiding under the sideboard all afternoon.) 'Poor little sod,' wailed Sonya, trying to cheer him up, ''tain't your fault if the Good Lord made yer a mangy runt.' (I don't know how she could complain when he bit her.)

There's still no sign of Barny emerging, although he could be seen through the parlour window wandering about. 'Well, I'm buggered,' Sonya declared after watching him a while. ''E *must* be poorly.' Then she made another comment, which I cannot repeat. (Funny thing, though. When Barny saw her peering at him, he shut his curtains. He won't answer the phone, either.) At least there's been no sign of the buxom beauty. And even after all this palaver, I'd still marry him tomorrow if he asked me.

There was a meeting about the Easter Fête. Sonya caused a row as usual, and had her stall confiscated and given to someone else. 'Right!' she said, storming out in a temper. 'Stick yer fête up yer bloody arse, an' see if I care!' I had a frantic word on her behalf, but the chairwoman was furious.

'If she can't conduct herself in a civilized fashion the whole fête could be brought into disrepute!' I'm glad she's not aware of Sonya's secondary line of employment, or she would never have agreed to give her another chance.

(My belly's sagging.)

Such excitement this morning! Maggie and Ethelbert had a letter to say they've been accepted as members of the Oswaldtwistle Ballroom Dancers' Association. They went off to town first thing, to buy their togs. But they were back in a couple of hours, looking heartbroken. 'You should see the prices, Jessy,' mourned the deflated Maggie, with tears in her eyes. 'There's no way we can afford to buy the proper gear.' And there was no way I could help them out from the money I make in the salon.

Lunchtime, when we were tucking into beans on toast, we all put our thinking caps on. It was Sonya who came up with the idea. 'Gerrin touch wi' Tipples,' she suggested. (If she'd been a dog, her tail would have been wagging.) 'I expect 'e gets stuff like that on 'is rounds.'

She was right. One phone call put the smile back on Maggie's face. 'Come in and have a look round,' said Tipples. 'I'm sure you'll be able to find what yer want.'

Off they went. And in no time at all they were back, with brown paper parcels tucked under their arms. After we shut the salon, Sonya, the kids and I were treated to a fashion display. Talk about Fred Astaire and Ginger Rogers! There was Maggie, bedecked in yards of bright pink tulle and silver slippers, and Ethelbert done up in a top hat, black drainpipe trousers and a great pair of black shiny boots. 'Gawd!' exclaimed Sonya. 'Look at the ol' sod. 'E's just like the artful dodger, ain't 'e?' It was all very entertaining, until they had a rather energetic go at the tango. When Ethelbert bent Maggie over, yards of stiff pink tulle went up in the air.

'I can see Maggie's bare bum,' shouted Wilhelmina, collapsing into fits of giggles. Then Ethelbert's wig fell off, when he got carried away in a frantic whirl, and after that there was no saving the situation. (I've no doubt they'll go on to win prizes in spite of Sonya's caustic comment: 'Oh, dear God, the gift to gi' us . . . to see ourselves as others see us.') At least it's given Maggie a better interest than standing on orange boxes in the market square, inciting folk to riot.

I've got my 'Strike it Lucky' form, to go on television with Michael Barrymore. But I can't get anybody to partner me. 'I can't go,' said Sonya, 'yer 'ave ter answer difficult questions.' Maggie and Ethelbert are too tied up in their ballroom dancing. And Barny's not talking to me. I'll have to send it back. (It's no wonder I'm suicidal.)

Ethelbert's in a fit because he can't find a matching pair of socks. 'Well, I put them in the washing machine!' roared Maggie. 'If they weren't in proper pairs when they came out, it's not my fault!' (I reckon the machine just gobbles them up.)

Friday, February 10th

Ethelbert's still sulking about his odd socks, and Maggie can't stop nagging. I got so fed up that I secretly taped her. When I played it back later, she shouted, 'Turn that radio off, Jessy. It's that bloody Thatcher woman!'

Sonya suggested we should all go out for a drink 'ter celebrate Maggie and Ethelbert's ballroom dancing career'. Without her knowing, I invited Tipples along. It was lovely to see the look on Sonya's face when he drew up in an ancient black car. It looked ready for the knacker's yard.

'I ain't setting foot in that monstrosity!' protested Ethelbert, backing away.

Sonya could see Tipples was offended. 'Don't be so

bloody daft, yer gurt lump,' she told Ethelbert, pushing him into the back seat, 'ye'll be as safe as 'ouses.' When he promptly went through the floor, she dragged him out. 'Ye've damaged it now!' she told him, shaking him by the scruff of his neck.

All was saved by Tipples' suggestion that he should take the car back to his yard, and we'd make our own way to the King's Head on foot. When Sonya dared to ask whether he wanted her to go with him, Tipples went all silly. 'No . . . it's all right,' he said, blushing scarlet.

'Sod yer, then,' snapped Sonya as he drove off. 'I shan't ask again!'

Anyway, it was a good night in spite of a bit of upset concerning the landlord's talking mynah bird. He's an evil-looking thing, with long drooping black feathers and small, vicious eyes, and he could teach navvies a thing or two about swearing, I'm sure. He lives in a huge green cage suspended from the ceiling by thick rusty chains, right over the pool table. 'The canny bugger referees every game,' claimed the landlord cockily.

'Gerraway,' snorted Ethelbert. 'What would a bloody bird know about a game o' pool, eh?' Straight away, he challenged Tipples to a match.

Almost immediately, the bird began heckling Ethelbert. 'Yer cheating, yer crafty bugger!' it screeched. 'Don't think I can't see what you're up to.'

It quite shattered poor Ethelbert's nerves. 'Tek the damn thing away,' he told the landlord, 'else I'll ring its scrawny neck.' He was quite beside himself – so much so that the landlord unhooked the cage and went out the back with it.

'Wonder where he's tekken the poor thing?' said Tipples, who, like the rest of us, had found the whole episode really amusing.

It was *me* who discovered where the landlord had taken the mynah bird, and it was not an ordeal I care to repeat ever again. It can be a terrifying experience when one is poised over the loo, ready to deliver, and out of the darkness comes a shriek of 'Who let the snake loose in the lavvy?' (I must have aged ten years.)

When we were making our way back home, I bumped into Barny at the corner of Victoria Street. 'You go on,' I told the others, 'I'll catch up in a minute.'

Barny seemed surprised to see me. When I asked whether he was feeling better, he put his hands on my shoulders and gently pushed me out of the light from the street lamp. When he had me pinned up against the wall, his arms about me and his warm breath fanning my face, I went weak at the knees. All those delicious feelings of wanting him flooded back to torment me. 'I've missed you, Jessy,' he said in that soft vibrant voice of his.

'I've missed you, too,' I murmured, revelling in the warmth of his body next to mine, 'but I could have come over if you'd wanted me to.' Brushing aside my words, he bent his head towards me, and of a sudden his mouth was on mine, his tongue doing unspeakable things to my nerve endings, and his body taut against me.

All manner of wonderful and exciting possibilities began rushing round in my mind. 'This is it!' I thought, feverishly clinging to him. 'At long last he's realized I'm a woman, he's a man, we're in love, and all things natural must surely follow.' Being in his arms, lost in the passion of his kiss, was a moment to cherish.

But, all too soon, the moment was gone. Drawing away and composing himself surprisingly quickly, Barny told me, 'I'll see you home. Then I'll away to my bed . . . I'm still not completely well.' He was suddenly aloof, withdrawn to where I couldn't reach him. That insurmountable barrier was there between us again.

'What *is* it?' I confided in Sonya later, as we walked up to fetch the kids from Winnie's mother's. 'Is it me? . . . is it something I've done to put him off?' When Sonya assured me that no, it was nothing *I'd* done, I felt instinctively that she was right. But when she murmured 'I've a feeling that you and Barny were doomed from the start' I felt she was definitely wrong. 'You've no call to say that,' I protested. 'We do love each other, you know . . . in spite of everything!' I added that it was our clash of business interests that was the core of all our problems.

'Ah,' she said, looking at me in a most peculiar fashion, 'would that it was so simple.' Beyond that she wouldn't be drawn, except to say quietly, 'Look, Jessy gal . . . I've a feelin' in me water that there's more to all o' this than meets the eye.'

'You think he's in love with that other woman, don't you?' I asked. 'You think he's going to dump me for her?'

'Not necessarily,' she replied, with a little chortle. 'First we need to establish that there *is* another woman!' (When Sonya's downed three pints, she gets these strange fancies.)

All the same, what *am* I going to do about the handsome Barny? Deep down, I suspect it *is* him who's been sending letters through his solicitor. And I suppose if I were to sell him my business and stop competing against him things might come right between us. But, much as I love him, I just can't do that. For the first time in my life, I've got my independence, and I love what I'm doing – and I've built it up into a steady little earner. I don't want to be rich, but I do need to keep what I've got. I'm proud of the salon. It's mine. Why should I close it down, or sell it to the competition, even if that competition *is* Barny? I lie awake at night, wondering whether he's deliberately teasing me and toying with my affections. Is he setting out to hurt me, because I stubbornly refuse to sell? Oh, I do wish he didn't mean so much to me. Life would be so much easier. (I've come to the conclusion that it's *men* who cause all the trouble in this world.)

Saturday, February 11th

What a day! We've been rushed off our feet in the salon, and didn't even get away for a cuppa until three o'clock. 'I've never known such a rush for a short back and sides,' I told Sonya, when we managed a minute to ourselves.

As usual, she had the answer. 'It's that new red-headed barmaid at the Rose and Crown,' she said. 'According ter Jack Tripp, she sends 'im boss-eyed when she flops 'er tits o'er the counter. One way or another she's med a big impression, an' all the fellas are fighting ter gerra look in.'

Ethelbert overheard. 'Huh! It don't bother me,' he said, swelling out his pigeon-chest. 'When ye've seen *one* tit ye've seen 'em all.' (I could have sworn Maggie deliberately tripped him up. But I can't be sure, because she was all over him when he staggered to his feet.)

Three hours it took the pair of them to get ready for their first ballroom session. Ethelbert's face was twisted in pain when he presented himself for inspection. 'Bloody Nora,' exclaimed Sonya, 'what's to do? Yer look like yer being strangled.'

'I am!' he groaned, grabbing front and back at his crutch. 'The Palais might 'ave plenty o' ballroom . . . but *I* bloody ain't!'

Maggie got out her sewing box. 'Tell me where it hurts most,' she ordered. 'I'll make a few nips and tucks, and you'll be as right as rain.'

'You keep away from me wi' them scissors,' Ethelbert

cried, hobbling behind the sofa where she couldn't reach him. 'It's *your* fault I'm in this predicament. I *telled* yer not to stitch up the opening in me Y-fronts.'

'I had to. It spoiled the line of your trousers,' argued Maggie. 'How can you look debonair with unsightly *bulges* everywhere?'

'Don't be so bloody daft, woman. It's *natural* fer a man to bulge in certain places.'

'That may be, Ethelbert Pitts,' declared Maggie, 'but *your* bulge has a nasty habit of growing out of all proportion when there's women about! If you haven't got the self-control to restrain it, then one must resort to needle and thread to keep it in place.' (A bit drastic, I thought. After all, Ethelbert hasn't got much *else* to be proud of.)

'Yer look lovely,' said Sonya, when they were both lined up for our opinion. Then she quickly rushed out to the scullery.

'You do,' I added. 'You look a real pair of professionals.' I also felt the need to escape to the scullery, where I found Sonya doubled up trying not to split her sides. 'Oh, you are cruel,' I said. 'It's not their fault if they have to dress in other folks' cast-offs.'

Maggie found us in a state of hysteria. 'I know,' she said, patting me lovingly on the back. 'I get emotional as well, bless your hearts.' (I'm ashamed of myself now.)

'Are they going to a fancy-dress?' asked Tom, when they'd gone out the door.

'Oh, boys are stupid,' chirped Miss Bossy-boots. 'They're doing a *charity walk!*'

When Sonya had gone home and the kids were in bed, I began getting ready for my date. Craig Forester was collecting me at nine o'clock, in time to catch the second showing of *Fatal Attraction*. I bathed and let my hair dry naturally into its new layer-cut. Then I put on my new cerise silk blouse, floral skirt and burgundy shoes. After that I dusted the minimum of make-up on to my face, with a touch of grey shadow over my eyes and a sweeping of dark mascara. The lipstick was the same shade as my blouse, and the end effect was quite pleasing. (It's a shame I've developed two more wrinkles – one either side of my mouth. But who wouldn't, if they had my lot to put up with?)

'You do look pretty, Jessy gal,' Sonya said, when she made her way back at ten minutes to nine. 'Gerroff an' enjoy yersel', darlin' . . . the kids'll be all right wi' me.'

I knew they would. But I had to be sure of one thing. 'Sonya, don't take offence,' I started, 'but . . .'

'It's all right, gal,' she interrupted, seeming to read my mind. 'I shan't fetch no menfriends round.'

'What's happened?' I needed to know. 'Have you managed to put them off for tonight?' (I knew that, as a rule, Saturday was her busiest night.) 'Oh, Sonya, that's really good of you . . . to cancel all your engagements just so you could mind the kids and let *me* have a night out.' (What a friend.)

'Naw,' she said with a weary sigh. 'I ain't cancelled nothing. It's them that's given *me* the elbow. The buggers are all off to try their luck wi' that red-haired barmaid from the Rose and Crown.' (The swines!)

What with one thing and another, plus the fact that it was nearly nine o'clock and my date hadn't turned up, Sonya and I got to talking. 'What is it, Sonya?' I asked, eager to help in any way I could. She looked such a pathetic figure, wedged in the chair, with her strawberry-blonde hair unusually unkempt, and her knees drawn up to that great bouncing chest.

'I dunno, gal.' She raised her pretty brown eyes, and I

was astonished to see them filled with tears. 'There comes a time when yer begin ter look at yerself . . . tek stock o' what ye've done wi' yer life so far. Well, I've been tekking stock o' my life, Jessy darlin', an' I don't much like what I see. Married to a Jack-the-lad when I were little more than a snotty-nosed kid . . . an' thrown on the rubbish dump when the bugger were fed up wi' me. Oh, I know I'm not the *only* poor sod whose dreams 'ave been pissed on . . . an' I know I won't be the last. But sometimes, Jessy gal, I feel cheated that things didn't turn out better.'

'In what way . . . better?'

'Well, just *better* somehow.' Of a sudden the twinkle came back to her eyes. 'It might all 'ave been different, y'know. There *was* a time when I were a decent sort, an' a certain feller took a real fancy ter me. Oh, yes . . . now, if I'd 'a wed *that* one when 'e asked me, things *would* 'a turned out better.' She lowered her eyes, and for a minute she fell into a quiet mood. I didn't speak or interfere, for I felt she was lost in memories of a time long gone. Memories that were both exquisite and painful. After a while, she gave an embarrassed little giggle. 'Y'know the feller, Jessy,' she said. (And I did.)

'It's Tipples, isn't it?'

'Aye. Tipples, the rag-a-bone merchant. Oh, 'e might look like some'at outta one of 'is own rag-bags. But 'e's a good man, Jessy . . .'ard-working an' reliable. I could 'ave 'ad that one, but I were too young, too blind, an' too bloody stupid. Now it's all too late. There's too much water gone under the bridge.'

I pointed out that it was never too late. That it was obvious to me she still loved him, 'and he probably still loves *you*, Sonya. After all, he's never married, has he? That must tell you *something*.'

But she didn't agree. 'All it tells me is that 'e thanked

'is lucky stars for a narrow escape. Tipples went ter pieces fer a while after I turned 'im down. Then, when 'e gorrimself together again, 'e poured all 'is energy into mekkin' a success of 'is rag-a-bone trade. Naw, Jessy gal . . . I missed me chance a long time ago. An' Tipples 'as never forgiven me. I wouldn't be surprised if, deep down, 'e 'ates the sight o' me.' There was no consoling her. Whatever I said made no difference. 'It's gone, darlin'. All gone wi' that water under the bridge.'

She swore me to secrecy regarding her feelings towards Tipples. 'I don't want 'im laughin' at me 'cause 'e's got 'is own back after all these years. Lerrim think I ain't got the time o' day fer 'im. At least that way I'll keep me pride . . . fer what it's worth, eh?'

So I can't tell Tipples how Sonya feels about him. And, in all truth, I don't really know how he feels about her. But when I think about how he went to a deal of trouble regarding his appearance the other night, I suspect he still has a light burning for Sonya. I'm not quite sure how to go about bringing the two of them together. And I would like to sort out my *own* disastrous love-life first. Here I am, head over heels in love with the dashing Barny . . . even though I suspect he might be the one trying to get me out of house and home. And I'm risking his wrath by going out with Craig Forester, who is, after all, nothing short of a complete stranger.

All in all, though, I do like him. We had a lovely time this evening. *Fatal Attraction* is really frightening. The married man has a fling on the side, and then, when he wants to finish it, the woman threatens his marriage and everything. It just goes to show how dangerous emotions can be – and how thin is the line between love and hate. (It's a bit like that with me and Barny.)

After the pictures, Craig took me for a meal at the

108

Tandoori (first time I've ever eaten Indian food). 'What would you like?' he asked, waving the menu in front of my face.

'Oh, I'll have the same as you . . . I like it *all*,' I lied. I didn't want him to think that, given the choice, I would have preferred fish and chips. When a plate full of pretty things in rich sauce arrived, I dived in with great gusto. 'It's one of my favourites,' I assured him, when he warned caution. Two minutes later I was in the ladies' room, my mouth under the cold water tap and smoke coming out of my ears.

'You're not a curry person at all, are you?' he said when I staggered back to the table. (It must have been my green face and red neck that gave the game away.)

After desperately soaking up a bottle of wine to cool my parched throat, I told him it was time I got back home (I could feel my legs going). He was every inch the gentleman as he escorted me to his van. 'Next time, we'll do it right,' he smiled. He really has got the nicest dark-blue eyes.

When we arrived in Casey's Court, he helped me out of the van, just as my favourite helmet sauntered by. 'Goot evening, ossifer,' I giggled, waving my handbag at him. I shut up quickly when he gave me a scathing glare before getting out his little black book. He's *already* got me down as the worst kind of criminal.

'Come on, sweetheart,' laughed Craig, hooking his arm round me and taking me gently to the door. Once there, and having the wall for support, I told him I'd thoroughly enjoyed the evening. Whereupon he bent his face to mine and, in the most tender loving manner, kissed me full on the mouth. It was quite a shock. Not full-blooded or paralysing like Barny's kiss . . . but warm and lovely, and comforting. 'You might be your own boss, Jessy,' he

109

murmured softly, 'but, deep down, you're crying out for somebody to take care of you. Somebody like *me*.' It was only after I'd said goodnight and fallen in the door that I realized three things. One was that he was absolutely right. The second was that Barny had been watching from his parlour window and seen us kissing. And most startling of all was that, in a roundabout way, Craig Forester had just proposed to me!

I was adamant that I had not indulged in too much wine, and I was not drunk. Sonya, however, was not of the same mind. 'Well, I'm buggered,' she chortled, as I lumbered into the back parlour. 'You're pissed!' After which, she must have emptied four gallons of black coffee down me. 'Gerroff ter bed,' she ordered, humping me up the stairs. 'I'll stay till Maggie an' Ethelbert gerr'ome. An' let's 'ope they ain't as pie-eyed as *you*, my gal, 'cause I ain't equipped ter deal wi' *three* drunkards!' (Oh, the shame.)

I can hear them talking downstairs, and I feel sick from all that coffee. But I'm not going out to the loo till they've all gone. I expect Sonya's telling them how I disgraced myself tonight, and I haven't got the courage to face Maggie . . . I know she'll give me a right dressing-down. So I'll wait till all's quiet on the western front, then I'll sneak down for a pee.

Funny thing, though. Lying here in the half dark, scribbling in my diary, I have to admit that I feel pleasantly partial to Craig Forester. He may not be as handsome or charming as Barny, and he's certainly not so well off, but, well . . . he's nice . . . sort of reassuring . . . and he's got a sense of humour. There is one little thing that niggles at me, though, and I can't for the life of me remember clearly. But I do seem to recall, somewhere between the curry and the wine, he actually questioned me about the salon . . . more about my distant relative, I suppose. Old Pops, who left me the little house in Casey's Court, together with the pitiful remains of his barber's business, cropped up in the conversation more than once, if my memory serves me right. 'Did you *know* old Pops?' I remember asking, at which point Craig Forester abruptly changed the subject.

The whole thing seemed a little disturbing. But I'm not sure of exactly what was said, though I have an uncomfortable feeling that, at one point, he expressed interest in *buying* the salon, should I ever decide to put it up for sale. And he's a builder by trade! I must have heard wrong. It's all this business about somebody trying to get their hands on it through that conniving solicitor. I'm beginning to suspect *everybody*, that's my trouble . . . even though I know deep down that it's *Barny* who's been giving me the hassle.

(I don't want a pee now. I'm too tired.)

Sunday, February 12th

How I dragged myself through this day I will never know. I've been staggering about with two left feet, a head like Bruno's punch-bag, and a mouth like a sewer. On top of which, that damned toaster finally exploded in a fit of crumbs and crust this morning. Tom's resorted to wetting his pants, and Wilhelmina's had fisticuffs with her best friend, freckled Winnie. 'She's trying to pinch my boyfriend!' madam sobbed into her roast beef at lunchtime.

'Well, if you will tamper with the male sex,' I told her firmly, 'you deserve all the heartache you get.'

'So do *you*, then!' she retorted. (Out of the mouths of babes and lunatics.)

111

Maggie's right. I *will* have to be more responsible, and set a better example to the kids. 'Give over,' Sonya said, when Maggie had gone off to the shops. 'You go out an' enjoy yersel', gal . . . life's too short to be miserable.' Then she saw Tipples and his cart ambling down the road. 'The bugger never even passed the time o' day,' she grumbled. After that, she spent all day slamming and banging about in a mood to frighten rats. Poor old Granny Grabber had her ears singed by the curling-brush, and little Larkin got thrown out for doing what comes naturally.

'Oh, Sonya,' I said, before rushing out to pacify the tearful Larkin, 'you didn't have to cause such a stink.'

''Tweren't *me* as caused the stink,' she argued. 'I've telled 'er . . . if she will insist on lerrin' go every time *I* bend over, then I ain't doin' 'er perms any more. Folks'll think it's *me* that's farting all over the place!'

'You mean "passing wind", don't you, Sonya?' (I must insist on proper standards at all times.)

'Naw! I mean what I said,' retorted Sonya, her mood darkening. 'If she comes back in this 'ere salon then *I'm* going on strike!'

At least the kids were in a better mood when Maggie and Ethelbert fetched them home from school. 'Maggie's promised to take us swimming on Saturday,' said Miss Clever-clogs.

'Yes, and I know a joke,' piped in the shorter version. 'D'you want to hear it?'

I daren't say no, in case he went off in a sulk again. 'Go on then . . . hurry up,' I said, carefully trimming round Marny Tupp's earhole.

'D'you know how this tribe of Indians got their name?'

he asked, looking cunning. When I told him that I had no idea, he went on to explain in great detail how the cavalry were hiding behind a wall, eating beans and throwing their empty cans over the top. When the wild Indians began creeping up on them, they kept cutting themselves on the tins and saying, 'Oh, my pawnee . . . my pawnee.' (Daft, isn't it?)

I did laugh, and I made a good job of pretending it was the best joke I'd ever heard, and for a minute Tom was really pleased with himself. Then Marny Tupp told him he'd never heard such a terrible story. Tom was so upset he barricaded himself in his room without any tea. 'Come on out, Tom,' entreated Ethelbert, 'and yer can play wi' my false teeth.' (He did as well. Ugh!)

The Council wallahs were round again today, equipped with tape measures, tripods and clipboards. Marny Tupp set his dog on them, and the woman from the tripe shop shouted in the street that they were not welcome round Casey's Court. Sonya was less polite. She hung her largest pair of bloomers out of the bedroom window, emblazoned in lipstick with the words 'Piss Of'. (She never could spell.)

Maggie waylaid one of them in the alley. He was a poor little bespectacled bloke with a nervous stutter. 'When am I going to get my bloody keys?' she demanded in her most frightening sergeant-major voice.

'You c-c-can't . . .' he started, shaking like a leaf. Convinced that he was going to say 'You can't have the keys', Maggie grabbed him by the scruff of the neck. When Ethelbert rescued him and fetched him into the salon, the poor thing was in a shocking state, trembling from head to toe and on the verge of a fit. It took four cups of tea and a nip of brandy before he could finish the sentence. 'You c-c-can't b-b-blame m-me!' he squeaked, clinging to his clipboard as if it was a life raft.

After they'd all gone, with their photos and measurements, Marny Tupp sent a leaflet round saying there'd be another meeting in the pub tonight. I didn't go, because I really can't see what good they're doing. 'What else *can* we do?' demanded Sonya. I told her I didn't know, because I'm not a leader of men. What I *was* sure of was that they would have a fight on their hands if they thought they could get past me to pull *my* house down! And, of course, I'd do all I could to help other residents of Casey's Court.

'But it's no use just talk talk talk, Sonya,' I told her, 'they never listen.' (I have sent another heartrending letter off to the Queen, though. I mean . . . how would *she* feel if they threatened to pull down Buckingham Palace? Where would the corgis live, for a start?)

We had to fetch Lucky from the dog-pound again. 'He's getting to be a real nuisance,' complained the inspector. 'He's on the constabulary's black list, y'know.' (Me and him both!)

Talking of police, my favourite helmet called in to see Sonya. Apparently they'd found her handbag, containing keys and make-up, down by Dingler's Dell. 'Oh aye,' he added with a funny look, 'we found a pair of black lacy drawers an' all.' (She says they were stolen. A likely tale!)

I went across to make my peace with Barny tonight, but he wasn't too pleased to see me. 'I haven't much time,' he said, 'I'm just off out on business.' I felt miserable and unwanted, but cheered up a bit when Craig Forester rang me at nine o'clock.

'I really love your company, Jessy,' he said, 'and I'd like to see you again.' Feeling slighted by Barny's treatment, I made so bold as to ask Craig round for a quiet meal on Saturday evening, which he jumped at. After-wards, I wondered whether I'd done the right thing. Oh, I like him and all that. He's very nice. But when you love somebody else, it's never a wise thing to encourage another man. Somebody's bound to end up getting hurt. All the same, I'm quite looking forward to seeing him again.

'Yer a dark 'orse, Jessy Jolly,' laughed Sonya, 'playin' one off agin the other, is it, eh? Can't say as I blame you, darlin' . . . us women 'ave ter use all the tricks in the book.' Then she went all serious. 'Don't set yer 'eart too much on that Barny Singleton, will yer?' When I asked her what she meant, she would only say, ''Cause I've a gut feeling that 'e ain't fer you . . . an' never will be.' (I expect she's referring to his bit on the side.)

'Don't pay too much attention to his flirting,' I told her. 'A handsome catch like Barny is bound to get more than his fair share of admirers. I've decided to forgive him and make a fresh start if he'll let me.' I was quite put out when she called me a 'bloody fool'. (Deep down, though, I know she's right.) I've invited her to dinner on Saturday. Now I've only got to persuade Tipples, and it could be the start of something big.

Tuesday, February 14th

Maggie and Ethelbert had a visitor from the Ballroom Dancers' Association. Apparently they've been invited to a long weekend in Spain, where they can dance, dine and mingle with members from far and wide. 'We're moving up in the world,' Maggie told Ethelbert, 'so you'd best get yourself smartened up, my man!' She promptly took him to town for a new pair of trousers. On their return he was ordered to put them on before being paraded in front of me, Sonya, and two perms from Rosamund Street. 'What do you think, Jessy?' asked Maggie. When I told her they were very smart but asked why he couldn't have a pair that came below the top of his boots, she gave me a scathing look and dragged him out. 'Wait till you're living on a pension,' she told me. 'You'll soon learn to cut your coat according to your cloth!' (Or your trousers, as the case may be.) 'What's more, you might be surprised to find that it isn't *what* you wear that matters . . . it's *how* you wear it.' (I wonder if poor Ethelbert's of the same mind.)

'Soddin' cheek,' Sonya called out. 'Ethelbert never wore his trousers like that afore 'e wed you. 'Ow would you feel with yer drawers at 'alf mast?'

She was gobsmacked when back came the answer, '*What* drawers? Who can afford *drawers* when they're living on a pittance?'

'Bloody Nora,' laughed Sonya, grabbing one of the perms from Rosamund Street. 'The ol' bat walks round wi' a bare arse!' (She has a lovely way of putting things.)

Wednesday, February 15th

I had a card from Tiffany today, postmarked Southampton. 'I'm off on my cruise,' it said. 'Perhaps the calming effect of the sea and the full moon at night will soothe my aching heart.' (Poor sod.)

Sonya came round about half-past eight. 'It's been a wearing day, gal,' she said, flopping into the chair and titivating herself. 'We're gerrin' more an' more kids comin' ter the salon. I can't abide cheeky bloody kids.' (I can't abide kids at all.) 'That soddin' Tiffany meks me

116

sick,' she snorted, taking a peep at the card. 'She sounds like a real drip . . . "soothe my aching heart" indeed! What *she* wants is a couple o' corns an' the wind up 'er arse. *That'll* give 'er some'at ter be going on with!' (I know when to keep my mouth shut.)

Seeing that I would not be drawn on her views concerning Tiffany, Sonya reluctantly changed the subject. 'Old Lenny Tremble breathed 'is last yesterday, I'm told . . . poor bugger.'

'Oh, that's a shame,' I said, feeling she required me to be sympathetic, even though I didn't know the fellow. 'I can't recall ever meeting him, though. Had he been ill a long time?'

'You wouldn't 'a known Lenny. 'E moved from these parts some time back . . . went to Chorley, I do believe. 'E were a reg'lar client o' mine, y'know. Now an' then 'e'd pop back fer a quick session of 'ow's yer father.' The mischievous twinkle returned to Sonya's eyes as she went on, 'Mind you . . . the poor ol' sod were well past it.'

'What . . . he wasn't well endowed, do you mean?' (Curiosity got the better of me.)

'Aw, no, gal. 'E 'ad is fair share did ol' Lenny Tremble,' she said with a vulgar chortle. 'The trouble is, gal . . . it needed ironing!' (I won't even ask!)

Thursday, February 16th

I sneaked an hour off today, when there was a suitable lull in the salon. 'Where yer going?' asked Sonya, blatantly adjusting her garter-tops in full view of the window. After lying that I was off to the dentist, I politely reminded her that if she wanted to hoist up her skirt and mess about with her undergarments, she ought not to

117

display the fact in full view of anybody who might happen by . . . not forgetting those who lived opposite and had done nothing to deserve such an eyesore.

'Yer cheeky sod!' she retorted, looking mortally wounded. 'There's folk willin' ter *pay* ter look at my arse. Did y'know there's women in Amsterdam who flaunt themselves afront o' the window day and night, eh? Paradin' their goods ter pull in the customers?'

'Sonya, this is *not* Amsterdam,' I reminded her. 'And this establishment is not offering the pleasures of the flesh to all and sundry. It's a little hair salon in a back street in Lancashire. Now, put yourself away and find something less tantalizing to do. There's enough hair lying on the floor to knit a rug . . . sweep it up, why don't you?'

She was most affronted. 'The trouble with you, Jessy Jolly,' she told me, 'is there's no sense of adventure in yer 'eart.' (She could be right.) When I was on my way out of the door, she yelled, 'If yer going ter the butcher's ter get the meat fer Saturday, get some'at juicy. We don't want none of yer spare ribs neither, 'cause I'm not spending 'alf the evening sucking on a bone.' Then, with an evil little chuckle, she added, 'I can think o' better things I could be doing.' (Dear Lord, teach me to close my mind to the images she creates.)

As it happened, I *did* call in the butcher's for a pound of best mince. Nobody makes better shepherd's pie than I do. (In fact, it's about the only dish I've fully mastered.) But I didn't make my way to the dentist – that had been just an excuse to get away on my own. Instead, I turned left at the bottom of Viaduct Lane, and went down to the end of Pump Street. In no time at all I was dithering outside Tipples' rag-a-bone warehouse. 'Well, if it ain't Mrs Jolly,' came a friendly voice from the vicinity of a grimy window. 'What can I do yer for, darlin'?'

Stepping into that cobbled yard was quite an experience. It was the first time I'd ever been there, and it was a real eye-opener. The yard itself was about twenty feet square, with a gutter running down the centre. The surrounding walls were in excess of eight feet high with, here and there, huge gaping holes which were open to the elements. When I expressed concern that he could easily be robbed, Tipples fell about laughing. 'If the buggers are so desperate that they need to rob *me*, they're welcome,' he said. Looking about, I could see what he meant. There wasn't a thing there worth more than a few pounds. But the *number* of things was staggering . . . rusty bikes, old car wheels, dilapidated prams, mowers without handles . . . all heaped one on the other until, in places, the tangled mounds reached high up above the wall. In one corner was a ramshackle wooden shed, from which the old mare's brown soulful eyes followed Tipples' every move. 'Bit of a mess, ain't it?' he chuckled, turning away towards the arched door which led to a large stone building. 'The best stuff's in here,' he explained as I followed. 'I keep *this* under lock and key.'

After seeing the chaotic mess out in the yard, I was astonished at the neat and careful layout in the vast warehouse. In fact, for a minute, I was lost for words. The place was *huge*, and at one time there must have been two storeys, because the ceiling was some thirty feet up. Against one wall were piled layer upon layer of woollies in a multitude of colours. The wall directly opposite the door was lined with shelves as far as I could have reached on tiptoe. The shelves were laid end to end with shoes and boots of all descriptions – ballet slippers, pumps, hob-nailed boots, walking brogues and stilettoes – all sizes and every colour of the rainbow. Around the perimeter of the remaining space were positioned several long metal racks, all hung with shirts, coats, dresses, blouses, and other articles of men's and women's clothing. 'I allus have 'em laundered afore I offer 'em fer sale,' Tipples explained proudly, before showing me a small annexe containing second-hand furniture and the like. 'I've put some good stuff aside fer when your Maggie gets 'er keys,' he said with a cheery smile. 'Found a posh commode as'll just fit Ethelbert's arse, too.'

'Where do you sleep?' I wanted to know, seeing nothing round me to indicate any living quarters. He seemed surprised that I should even ask such a stupid question. 'Why, with me old faithful o' course,' he said. 'Where else?' (Where else indeed!)

Without further ado, he showed me how he'd partitioned the shed in two – equally shared between himself and the old mare. 'We're both very comfortable,' he said, indicating the calor-gas stove, washbasin and narrow brass bed over which was a double cupboard 'for me pots an' pans'.

In a minute he had me seated on an upturned bucket, with a mug of good strong tea in my hand. 'Now then, darlin',' he asked, supping at his own mug, then running finger and thumb across his mouth. 'What's fetched yer to *my* neck o' the woods?'

Of a sudden I felt embarrassed. He was not aware that I knew of his past relationship with Sonya. How was I to start? Would he throw my invitation back at me, if he even *suspected* that Sonya would be there as well? My courage was fast deserting me. I was on the point of asking whether he had any good working televisions when my chance presented itself. ''Ere! It's nothing ter do with Sonya, is it? I mean, yer not here because some'at's happened ter Sonya?' He was quite perturbed.

Before I lost my nerve I blurted out, 'No, of course

120

not. Sonya's fine. In fact . . . I'd like you to come to dinner on Saturday, Tipples. You . . . and Sonya?'

For a long time he gave no answer. Then, with his eyes lowered to the ground, he asked in a quiet voice, 'Does she know yer asking *me* as well?'

'Of course!' I lied (God forgive me). 'She's thrilled at the idea.'

'Yeah?' He looked up to fix me with those merry green eyes, which were now wide with surprise. 'Is that a fact? Well I never!' He really did have a handsome smile beneath all those whiskers. 'I'm very grateful, Jessy.' Then, suddenly, the smile had disappeared and his whole manner had changed. 'I'd like to accept yer kind invitation . . . but no, I can't.' No amount of persuasion would change his mind, either.

'Don't say for definite, Tipples,' I begged him. 'Think it over before you decide, please.'

'Aye, all right, darlin'. I'll think on it, but you'll find the answer's still the same. Y'see . . . I med a fool o' meself a long time ago with Sonya . . . thought the world of her, I did, and I would have done *anything* for her. But she didn't want me. Didn't want me then an' doesn't want me now.' He looked so directly at me that I felt uncomfortable, like the fibber I was. 'I don't believe she *does* know yer asking me along,' he said with a sad little smile, 'but I'm grateful for what yer trying to do . . . she has a good friend in you, Jessy. But I've found out that loving somebody can be a painful thing if you ain't loved back. No . . . best let bygones be bygones, when all's said and done.'

'Are you saying you *don't* love her any more?' I asked unashamedly. 'Have you no feeling at all for Sonya?'

'I ain't saying I have . . . an' I ain't saying I haven't. All I'm saying is that I've been hurt once . . . badly. An'

I've no intention o' being hurt agin. I'm content enough
. . . me an' the old faithful.'

'Sonya really is fond of you, Tipples. I *know* she is.'

'No . . . it's all too late, darlin'. We had our chance
. . . an' we lost it,' he said, shaking his head and getting
to his feet. 'Don't you feel badly, though. It were worth a
try.'

I *did* feel badly. I felt close to tears.

But Tipples was generous, because I went home with a
bucket to catch any tears, and a rusty old iron, a framed
picture of Queen Victoria and a rat-trap (unfortunately
not big enough for the Barny variety).

When I got back to the salon, Sonya stared at me wide-
eyed. 'I thought you went ter the dentist, gal? Looks
more like ye've been rummaging about in the bloody tip.'
When I lied that there had been a jumble sale on at the
vicarage, she put her hands on her ample hips and rolled
her brown eyes to heaven. 'Ain't *nothing* safe no more?'
she asked. 'The vicar's meant ter dish out absolution, not
piss-pots an' rat-traps.' Then she immediately clapped her
hand over her mouth, looking suddenly mortified. 'Sorry,
Lord,' she mumbled, 'but yer did slip up when yer gave
that prat the job, yer must admit.' (She's got a thing
against the vicar, ever since he came to her house and
asked if she wanted him to 'exorcise the devils of sin who
abide here'. He went off in a huff when she showed him
the door and pointed out that Ethelbert didn't live there
any more.)

Granny Grabber's been arrested. Apparently she was reported for standing outside Woolworths and dropping pound coins to the pavement. When unsuspecting shoppers stooped to pick them up, she pounced on them from behind, clutching at a handful of their squashy bits and squealing with delight, 'Bet you thought your luck had changed.'

I was appalled. 'Where on earth does she get the idea that folk enjoy being grabbed from behind?' I commented to Sonya.

'Dunno, gal,' she chuckled, 'an' I don't care. What I want ter know is where on earth does she get pound coins ter chuck on the pavement, eh?' (Come to think of it, she *is* an old-age pensioner. She must save up for weeks for her little pleasures.) They soon let her go, though. It seems she had the station in an uproar and two rather well-endowed constables will be on sick leave for some time.

When Granny Grabber's in one of those moods, *nobody's* safe. 'You keep away from that end of Casey's Court,' I told Tom. 'And don't let Lucky loose in that vicinity.'

'Oh, that's all right, Mam,' he said, matter of fact. 'He *likes* it.' (No wonder he's been hobbling lately.)

Maggie and Ethelbert have gone off to Spain for their long weekend. 'Have a lovely time, the pair of you,' I said, seeing them off on the coach.

'Oh, we intend to,' retorted Maggie, grabbing Ethelbert by the scruff of the neck and hoisting him over the step. 'Don't we, chichicoo?' she smiled.

'You are a caution, Maggie,' he said. (By the look on his face, he'd already been promised his treats.)

'You *have* brought a good supply, haven't you, cherub?' Maggie asked him.

'Course I 'ave!' he retorted, showing her his three clean hankies. (Shame on me for dirty thoughts.)

It's amazing how quiet the house seems without Maggie and Ethelbert. I miss them, but I'll be glad for their sake when they get the house next door. We won't be forever under each other's feet, but we'll be within shouting distance should we feel the need.

Sonya and the kids came with me after tea to collect jumble for the Easter Fête's white elephant stall. We quite filled the old pram lent by freckled Winnie's mother. There was a complete set of encyclopaedias, a wilted wandering-jew plant in a lovely ceramic pot, two sets of false teeth, a bicycle pump, two floral dresses – one size 12, the other more like a tent – and an old brass car horn with a rubber ball at one end. Sonya would insist on squeezing the thing every two minutes. The noise it made was horrendous. By the time we got back to Casey's Court every female dog in Oswaldtwistle was trailing behind us. Behind them were the randy dogs, and last of all were multitudes of kids. (I felt like the Pied Piper.) 'I've changed me mind, Jessy,' Sonya chuckled, pointing the horn at a passing geriatric who nearly had a fit when she let go full blast. 'I want to man the white elephant stall . . . it's fun, ain't it?'

Saturday, February 18th

We weren't too busy in the salon today, which was just as well, because the only thing I had on my mind was the dinner and whether I would do my guests justice. This was my very first stab at entertaining since I left the south,

124

and my one hope was that it should all go really well. 'Three's an odd number,' said Sonya teasingly. 'Why don't yer invite Barny Singleton? I'd like the chance ter get the bugger sozzled, so's I can find out what little games 'e's up to.' I soon put paid to *that* idea. Goodness me! As if I hadn't got enough problems with Barny as it is. I don't think he'd ever forgive me if he suspected I was entertaining another man – however innocently. (Then again, I wonder whether he'd even care?) All the same, I've done my best to make amends between us. Now it's up to him.

A new fellow's moved into No. 18. The old lady who bought it from the Council has sold up and gone into an old folks' home. 'I've lived in Casey's Court these sixty years,' she told the woman from the tripe shop, 'but I ain't got much longer on God's earth, and I want to spend me last few seasons in peace and quiet.' (I know how she feels!)

'That new bloke's a funny-looking geezer, Jessy gal,' remarked Sonya, as she turned from the window where she'd spent the last hour checking every item that came out of the removal van. 'I 'ope 'e ain't gonna be no trouble, else we'll soon 'ave the bugger on 'is way.' When I asked what she meant by calling him a 'funny-looking geezer' she launched into great detail about his small military moustache and his authoritative bearing. 'It wouldn't surprise me if 'e ain't related ter the rent man,' she said. 'That one's a snot-rag as well.' When I pointed out that she mustn't judge by first impressions, she told me he had conducted the installation of his furniture 'like a bloody sergeant-major'. And how could I explain the fact that he had 'two sets o' drums, four trumpets, three French horns, two trombones, a set of cymbals an' two o' them big oompah things'? I suggested that perhaps he was a mender of musical instruments.

All the same, she had me curious, peeking from behind the net curtains like one of those nosy cows I can't abide. 'What are you two gawping at?' demanded the woman from the tripe shop, who came back for her handbag. 'Lose me head if it weren't screwed on,' she laughed. 'Oh! That reminds me. I'd best take a packet o' them doodahs . . . the fine gossamer ones in the gold packet. My fella didn't care much for them extra-long . . . says it were awkward with three inches hanging loose at the end.' Tutting loudly, she made for the condom stand. 'Honestly! He'll be wanting made-to-measure next.' Then she joined us at the window. 'I said, what are you two gawping at? Oh, that new chap at No. 18, is it? Funny looking bloke if you ask me. And did y'know he's got two sets o' drums, four trumpets, three French horns, two trombones, a set o' cymbals, two big oompah things . . . and half a dozen tambourines?'

'Tambourines? We never saw no tambourines, did we, Jessy gal?' said Sonya, quite put out.

'Aye, well . . . *I* saw 'em. Lord only knows *what* he's up to, with a brass band in his parlour.' Of a sudden she was eyeing Sonya in a most peculiar fashion. 'Hey! He's not one o' *your* clients, is he? I don't mind turning a blind eye to *one* o' my neighbours clattering and banging about at all hours, getting up to heaven knows *what* debauchery. But, I tell you now, I shall draw the line if some other Jack-the-lad thinks he can get away with it.'

'Y'reckon, do yer?' asked Sonya, looking for trouble, I thought. 'And what will yer do then, eh?'

The woman from the tripe shop made for the door. 'What will I *do*? Well, I shall demand a rates rebate,

126

that's what!' Then, hastily paying the money for her purchase, she hurried out and away up the street.

'Silly old cow,' snorted Sonya. 'Whatever does she think somebody in *my* business could do with brass instruments, eh?' A wicked smile spread slowly across her face. 'Oh, I dunno though. Come ter think of it, I might tickle some lucky bloke's fancy wi' a pair of cymbals.' (It doesn't bear thinking about.)

'Get off home with your warped little mind,' I told her with a chuckle. 'I've to get the kids their tea, then wash and bed. There's a shepherd's pie to make and a trifle to prepare. Go on . . . I'll see you later.'

'Right then. I'll be back about eight o'clock, so's I can give you a hand before your fancy man arrives.'

'Craig Forester is *not* my fancy man.'

But she would have none of it. 'If you don't fancy him, he fancies *you*, my gal. An' if yer ask me, 'e's a safer bet than Barny Singleton.' When I asked her why she was so set against me and Barny getting together, she gave me a strange look. 'Because I can't see it ever 'appening, gal,' she said. 'There's men, an' there's . . . men. An' Barny Singleton can't mek up 'is bloody mind.' With that, she left, leaving me totally confused. Still, that's our Sonya . . . talks in riddles, she does. But her heart's in the right place, bless her.

I don't know what it is about Sonya, but wherever *she* is there's trouble. It was a funny evening to start with. First of all, the raspberry jelly in my trifle stubbornly refused to set, and I had to rush out for a tub of ice cream and a tin of pear halves. Then, just as I thought the kids were settled for the night, Tom woke up in the middle of a nightmare. 'They're coming to get me,' he cried. (I wish they would!)

The very evening when I wanted my hair to look its

127

best, it just hung like a blanket in the rain. And when Sonya turned up, she resembled one of those painted dolls you shy coconuts at. 'Oh, Sonya!' I moaned, reluctantly letting her in. 'Did you have to use so much rouge? Just once, couldn't you have gone for the demure and sophisticated look?' (I was in a snotty mood, and, deep down, I still had the faintest hope that Tipples might turn up.)

'If yer don't like me, gal,' replied Sonya – quite rightly so – 'then yer can bloody well lump it! I ain't the "demure and sophisticated" kind, so there's no use pretending. Yer dress up what ye've got in the best way yer can. There ain't no point in fooling the customers, is there, eh?'

'*What* customers?' I asked. 'This is a dinner party, not a butcher's shop!'

'I knows that, don't I, gal,' she retorted with a little laugh, 'but yer never know 'ow yer luck can change on the way 'ome. Anyway, if yer think *this* end is well and truly powdered, yer should see the *other*.' (Not me!)

By the time Craig arrived, Sonya had managed to calm me down, and forgiven me for being so awful. 'Ye've done us proud, me darlin',' she said, looking at the table we'd brought in from the scullery, which was beautifully bedecked with a pretty lace cloth, pink twisted candles and my best glasses. 'Oh, an' *you* look a treat as well,' she added, grabbing me in a bear-hug, then stepping back to give me the once-over. 'That blue dress really suits yer . . . an' what a clever idea ter match up the earrings an' shoes. That soft blue really brings out the autumn highlights in yer hair. Now *you* . . . well, talk about being demure and sophisticated . . . it's *you*, ain't it? You an' me, Jessy gal, we're like a slice of best sirloin an' a bit o' scrag-end.' (How can you not love her?)

'Don't talk rubbish, Sonya,' I told her. 'You're the salt

128

of the earth, and nobody ever had a kinder heart. If the
end of the world was nigh, and Noah had to choose
between us, he wouldn't even hesitate. He'd take *you*
into the ark and leave *me* to drown like the worthless
thing I am.'

'You ain't!' she laughed. 'I saw yer open that tin o'
pears like a good 'un. What's more, everything went into
the Ark in *twos*. I'd need at least half a dozen fellas ter
keep *me* amused.' When I told her she was incorrigible,
she said, 'There's no need to resort to foul language.' We
were still laughing when Craig knocked on the door. 'I'll
lerrim in,' she said. 'You mek yersel' look attractive.
Drape yersel' o'er the settee or some'at.'

Craig looked very fetching in a cream-coloured shirt
and grey suit. The minute his navy-blue eyes smiled at
me, I went all of a flutter inside. Funny that, because I
don't think of Craig in the same way I think of Barny. It's
more of a platonic thing between me and Craig, whereas
I turn to jelly every time Barny takes me in his arms
(which, I have to admit, is not as often as I'd like).

We'd just sat down to start the meal when there came
another knock on the door. '*I'll* gerrit,' Sonya cried,
jumping up from the table with a fierce look on her face.
I had an awful feeling that she thought it might be Barny,
and was preparing to send him away with a flea in his ear.

'No, I'll go,' I told her quickly, heading her off. When
I opened the door, who should be there but Tipples, the
rag-a-bone man.

'I've changed my mind, Jessy,' he said, looking embarrassed. 'I'd like to accept yer kind invitation . . . if it's not
too late?'

'Of course it's not too late.' I was really pleased to see
him. 'Come on through. Sonya will be so pleased.' He
looked really attractive, with his long reddish hair drawn

129

back into a thin brown shoelace and his beard all clean and fluffy. He was wearing smart green cords and a black polo-neck jumper.

'I don't know how to dress proper,' he said. 'I'm not used ter dinner parties and the like.' His green eyes twinkled when I assured him that he looked very handsome and it didn't matter *what* he wore.

'I'm just glad you decided to come,' I told him.

If *I* had been surprised at Tipples turning up, Sonya nearly choked on her wine when I brought him through. 'Bloody Nora!' she muttered. 'What's *'e* doin' 'ere?' Her choice of words was unfortunate, because from that minute Tipples was on his guard. *I* knew she was pleased to see him, because I'd learned to read her moods very well. But Tipples wasn't quite sure what to make of her, and occasionally he would lapse into an uncomfortable silence.

All in all, though, everybody enjoyed the meal, and there was a deal of interesting conversation. Craig seemed to sense a certain atmosphere between Sonya and Tipples, and he went out of his way to draw them into the proceedings. Unfortunately, not knowing their past delicate relationship, he dropped a brick when he jokingly asked, 'How come you never got married then, Tipples . . . found out what devious devils women are, did you?'

Having drunk a little too much wine, Tipples launched into a long and detailed account of 'women who don't know when they're well off . . . who'd rather shack up with a no-good rat than wed a fella who really loves them'. In no time at all, Sonya was at his throat.

'What woman wants ter wed a bloke who can't stay in one place fer more than five minutes, eh? An' can yer blame 'er if she wants some'at more than a bloody rag-a-bone waggon ter ride ter church on?'

Seeing the two of them were getting hot under the collar, I persuaded Sonya to help me in the scullery and leave the men to chat a while.

After a few minutes, during which we could hear their murmuring voices, everything went quiet. Almost at once came the sound of the front door quietly closing. Craig then poked his head round the scullery door, his face a picture of remorse. 'I'm afraid Tipples has gone,' he said. 'He asked me to apologize, and to thank you, Jessica, for a lovely meal. Unfortunately, he feels he's spoiled your dinner party with his ungracious comments.'

Leaving Sonya to get the coffee, I ran out on to the pavement, but there was no sign of Tipples. Coming back into the parlour, I was all set to give Sonya a quiet little lecture on how not to hurt the one you love. But she looked so upset I gave it a miss.

Later, after I'd seen Craig off the doorstep, where he kissed me in that warm, pleasant way he has, I went back into the parlour, to find Sonya seated at the table with her head in her hands and a puzzled look on her face. 'Well, I'm buggered,' she said, staring towards the doorway. 'What a turn-up fer the books. I *never* would 'a thought it, Jessy gal!'

'Well, it was partly your fault,' I reminded her. 'Tipples came here in all good faith . . . with his heart on his sleeve . . . and you went out of your way to argue with him.' I was really cross, and I let her know it.

Imagine my surprise when she said, 'No, I don't mean *Tipples*! I mean that Craig Forester. D'yer know, Jessy gal, I'd 'a sworn 'e were a good 'un. But, when you went out after Tipples, I put me 'ead round the parlour door ter ask whether he wanted a biscuit or some'at . . . an' d'yer know, Jessy gal, the thieving sod were rummaging about in the stairs cupboard.' I couldn't believe it, and I

131

said so in no uncertain terms. But I had to stop and think when Sonya pointed out how he had insisted on going upstairs in my place to check the kids. 'An' what about going out ter the lavvy *five* times, eh? Yer can't tell me that's natural.' Come to think of it, she's right. What's more, he was like a cat on hot bricks all evening . . . wandering up and down, continually asking questions about old Pop . . . was anybody with him when he died? What were his last words? He wanted to know all manner of things concerning the house. Had there been any structural alterations since I moved in? He was most interested in the fact that I'd found a tin full of worthless papers and things stuffed up the chimney. At one point I even thought he was about to thrust his head up there to have a look.

'What's the bugger up to?' Sonya wanted to know.

'Don't be silly, Sonya,' I said, managing a feeble smile. 'Craig Forester's a nice fellow. He's not up to anything.'

All the same, it's been a very disturbing evening, what with one thing and another. (Hurry home, Maggie. All is forgiven.)

Sunday, February 19th

It poured down all morning and well into the afternoon. Tom and Wilhelmina gave me a rotten headache, moaning on and on because they couldn't play out. 'Good job when Maggie gets back tomorrow,' snapped Miss Know-all. 'At least *she* plays cards with us!'

Tom chipped in with his little bit too. 'I'd rather play with Ethelbert, though, 'cause *he* doesn't go off in a sulk when we beat him, does he, Willie?'

His sister was most affronted. 'Mam! Stop him from

132

calling me "Willie" . . . my name's Wilhelmina. Else I'll run away.' (Please, God.)

Sonya popped round after lunch. 'Cor, bloody Nora!' she shouted from the passageway, where she shook her mac and sprayed the walls. 'It's raining cats an' dogs out there. The weatherman says it's gonna piss down all day.' When I asked her to watch what she said, because the kids were about, she totally misunderstood, telling them with a laugh, 'Not daft are ye, kids, eh? Yer can see fer yersel' that it's pissing down, can't yer?'

Madam regally informed her that 'Mam meant that you mustn't use bad words in front of us, Sonya. She's a spoilsport.'

'That's right,' said Tom. 'She don't like it when you say "pissing down".' (I don't know why I bother.)

We had a terrible catastrophe before I could escape to the safety of my bed (my nerves have gone).

About half past two, when the rain finally stopped, Tom went outside to spend a penny. 'You be sure and close that lavvy door properly afterwards,' I told him.

'And tell him not to splash all over the seat,' interrupted Miss Bossy-boots. 'If *I* can do it neatly, he should be able to, because *he's* got a thingy.' (I just ignored her.)

I'd made us all a drink and was just handing Sonya her cup of tea when there came a terrified scream, accompanied by a loud clatter. 'Gawd luv us!' exclaimed Sonya, jumping up and knocking the cup flying. 'What the 'ell were that?'

Bossy-boots knew. 'Tom's fell down the lavvy,' she laughed, running to the back door. 'I *bet* he has. I bet he's fell down the lavvy, Mam.' (Knowing how thoughtless kids are, I wasn't surprised.)

There was no sign of Tom as the three of us rushed down the yard towards the lavvy. The flags beneath our feet were still wet and slippery. 'Don't 'ang on ter me, Wilhelmina,' Sonya warned, 'else ye'll 'ave us *all* arse over tip!'

In a minute, the lavvy door was flung open to expel the dazed culprit, together with a torrent of water, which appeared to be gushing from above the cistern. 'It wasn't *my* fault,' wailed Tom, tears falling down his guilty face, 'I was only pulling myself up to see where the chain went, and that long black thing broke.' He then collapsed into a volley of heartrending sobs and tore off up the yard.

'The little sod,' cried Sonya, as he disappeared into the house. ''E's been swinging on the bloody pipe, an' 'e's snapped it in two.' She pointed to where the end of the gushing pipe was wedged up the corner near the cistern. 'We shall 'ave ter stop it, gal,' she said, 'else ye'll be flooded out an' no mistake. D'yer know where yer stop-cock is?' When I admitted I had no idea, she told me I was a useless cow. 'Gerrin an' fetch an umbrella,' she ordered Wilhelmina, who thought it was all some wonderful adventure. 'I shall 'ave ter try an' join them pipes up agin . . . oh, an' fetch that big crepe bandage outta the kitchen drawer. Go on! Move yer bloody arse, young 'un. I ain't sticking me 'ead in there wi'out yer mam 'olds an umbrella o'er me. I've 'ad enough o' gerrin' wet fer one day!' When I asked whether we shouldn't just close the door and call a plumber, she turned on me. 'Fer an intelligent woman, yer do talk bloody daft, Jessy,' she ranted (my self-confidence was completely shattered). ''Ow the 'ell can we get near enough ter grab the door an' pull it shut, wi'out gerrin' soaked ter the skin, eh? An' even if we *could* manage ter shut the door, *where* d'yer think the water would go, eh? Yer can't stop a flood by closing a sodding *door* on it. An' there ain't no plumbers on a Sunday!' (She has a way of looking at you that makes you squirm.)

When the umbrella and bandage were duly brought by the unusually helpful Wilhelmina, Sonya took complete charge of operations. 'See if yer can manage ter 'old that brolly o'er me 'ead while I climb on the lavvy an' join the pipe up.' When I assured her that I was quite capable of managing such a simple task without her abusing me, she said nothing. But the glare she sent in my direction would have slain Goliath.

What followed was a nightmare I shall never forget. First of all, I gingerly advanced with the open brolly to fend off the frightening torrent of water now spewing from the pipe. Having cleverly positioned it so that the water was deflected *away* from Sonya and into the far wall, she clambered up on the lavvy, bandage at the ready. 'Don't you move!' she yelled. 'Else ye'll 'ave the pair on us drowned.' With the water now pouring down the wall and filling my shoes, the door began to move with the weight of the water behind it.

'Hurry up, Sonya,' I yelled frantically, pushing back the door with my shoulders, and stretching my aching arms even higher with the brolly. All seemed to be going well.

''Old on, gal,' cried Sonya, 'I've pushed 'em together. Now . . . if I can get this bandage round ter 'old it.'

I sighed with relief. Sonya struggled to contain the water. And Wilhelmina suddenly lurched forward, clinging to me like a monkey and screaming, 'A rat! There's a *rat* in the water!' From then on it was utter, unholy chaos. Being terrified of rats, and with the brat wrapped round me with its legs under my chin, I did the only thing *anybody* would do in the circumstances. I leapt on to the lavvy and threw my arms about Sonya. I could hear myself screaming, but I couldn't stop it.

'There's a *rat*!' I shouted. 'A *rat*!' As if that wasn't enough, the brolly fell over our shoulders and Sonya had to let go the pipe.

'Yer bloody lunatic!' she yelled (amongst other choice words). 'Gerroff! Get down!' She was spluttering now on account of the deluge of water pouring down on us. 'The only bloody rats 'ere is you an' me . . . a pair o' *drowned* rats!' With that, she began struggling, her leg went down the lavvy, one of the brolly spokes stabbed Wilhelmina in the arm, and I slipped to the ground, straight into a rat-infested fast-flowing river. Screaming like a banshee, I'm ashamed to say I up and fled, with the water pouring out of my drawers and the brat hanging on to my tail.

I was still in a state of shock when Sonya staggered in, wet and bedraggled, with the remains of the brolly crushed in her fist. 'I've never seen owt like it in all me born days,' she said, collapsing into a chair and glowering at the bemused Tom, who had watched the entire proceedings from a safe distance. 'An' they say *I'm* a useless prat.' (*Who* said that?) Without another word, she handed the tattered brolly to Tom, looked at me as if I was something despicable, shook her head and left.

'She's not friends to you now, is she?' asked Wilhelmina with wide frightened eyes. 'I *did* see a rat though . . . honest.' (She did indeed. I was looking right at it.)

Monday, February 20th

We've all got coughs and sneezes; all except Tom, of course. The plumber said the joint in the pipes was rotten, and it was a good job it didn't happen when one of us was *sitting* on the lavvy. (I didn't dare tell him that, because of my shameful cowardice, poor Sonya was actually *in* it.

136

Well . . . we *all* were.) We're friends again, though. 'Yer a walking bloody disaster,' Sonya said. She didn't believe me when I argued that I hadn't been till I met *her*.

Maggie rang to say the plane had been delayed, and they didn't expect to get back till Tuesday morning. We were all a bit disappointed. 'I want to see what she's brought us,' moaned Tom.

'And *I'm* going to tell them that you broke the pipe in the lavvy. Then you won't get a present,' warned Wilhelmina. (I let them fight. I'm past caring.)

Sonya had another run-in with the buxom beauty. 'Saw the bugger sneaking outta Barny Singleton's just now,' she said, coming into the parlour about nine P.M., out of breath and carrying what looked like a shoe. 'I chased the tart outta Casey's Court, afore she gave me the slip,' she explained. 'An' she lost this.' She brandished the red object in front of my nose. It *was* a shoe, a very fashionable, high-heeled and expensive thing. But I had to agree with Sonya when she concluded, "Ave yer ever seen such a bloody gurt big thing in all yer life, Jessy gal, eh? It looks more like a *barge* than a shoe, don't it? Mind you,' she mumbled, a thoughtful look on her face, 'I can't say I'm all that surprised . . . if me suspicions turn out to be right.' At least I *think* that's what she said (Barny really is a swine). It must have been an hour later when the phone rang. 'Leave it to me,' ordered Sonya, rushing to answer it. 'I expect it's the geriatric wanderers got theirselves into a pickle somewhere, an' want fetching 'ome.'

I was kept in suspense for a few minutes while she picked up the receiver, said 'Yes?' in a somewhat sharp manner, and then, after a short silence on her part (when presumably whoever it was on the other end held a one-way conversation), she suddenly told them in a curt and frosty voice to 'Piss orf!'

137

'I take it that *wasn't* the "geriatric" wanderers in a pickle, then?' I laughed, assuming the call had been one of those cranky folk.

'No,' she said, going out to the scullery to put the kettle on, 'it were a wanderer of *another* sort . . . an' if yer ask me, 'e's in a greater pickle than Maggie or Ethelbert ever could be.' When I questioned her further, she told me, 'It were that bag o' tricks from across the road.'

'*Barny*, you mean?' I was on my feet in a hurry, remembering how she'd spoken to him. 'Oh, for goodness sake, Sonya . . . how will Barny and I ever get back together again if you keep interfering like that?' (Sometimes your friends can be your worst enemies.) She wasn't perturbed, though, as she sauntered back into the parlour.

'I'm only thinking o' you,' she said, offering me a biscuit out of the barrel. 'That Barny's a wrong 'un. I'm telling yer, 'e'll only fetch yer a deal of 'eartache, gal. Yer better off wi'out 'im.' When I told her that she should allow *me* to be the best judge of that, she snatched the biscuit barrel away, slammed it on to the mantelpiece and stormed off up the passageway. 'Yer a silly arse, Jessy Jolly,' she shouted, 'a fool ter yersel'. I'm determined to catch your precious Barny wi' 'is trousers down, you see if I don't. An' if I'm *right* . . . well, ye'll see wharra narrer escape ye've 'ad!'

I rang Barny back straight away. 'It's me, Jessy,' I said, preparing to explain.

'Oh yes?' he snorted. 'Well, *you* can piss off now!' (I sometimes feel I can't go on.)

We were rushed off our feet from opening time. Sonya was frosty all day. And *I* wasn't going to be the first to speak! Little Larkin acted as go-between for a while, but it all proved too much for the poor wee thing . . . especially when I asked her to relay a request to the pouting Sonya: 'Tell her your hair frizzes if it's given too much perm' (I *know*, because *I* normally do Larkin's hair).

'Oh yeah?' interrupted Sonya with a sneer. 'Well you tell '*er*, Larkin me ol' flower, that *I'm* the one doing your 'air today. An' I shall do it the way *I* see fit. If the mood teks me, I shall not only frizz yer '*air*, but yer eyebrows an' ear'oles as well!' I shall never forget the sight of Larkin when she fled past me and out of the door, the towel still round her neck and half her head in rollers. If the tune she was playing was anything to go by, she was in a state of mortal terror. At least it broke the ice between me and Sonya, when she laughingly asked whether it would be all right to 'go an' pacify the poor little cow'. Of course, I told her she must.

At least Maggie and Ethelbert had enjoyed themselves, in spite of a few hiccups. 'Ethelbert can't sit down,' declared Maggie, fixing him with her beady eye.

'Oh, dear,' I said sympathetically, seeing how red and sore his arms were from too much sun, and recalling the time I burnt the back of my legs when sunbathing. 'You shouldn't expose yourself all at once. They say do a bit at a time.'

'Oh, aye,' agreed Maggie. 'I warned the old fool. But he wasn't satisfied with "doing a bit at a time", oh no.' Here she slapped his cap clean off his head in a fit of anger. 'He had to expose it all at once . . . every horrid square inch . . . down on the nudist beach!'

'Be fair, Maggie, precious,' argued Ethelbert the pink, 'I gave them poor old dears a rare treat.' He looked really pleased with himself.

'You think so, do you?' demanded Maggie. 'And what about the two you gave a heart attack, eh? What! The sight of you and your burnt offerings were enough to send them running in *all* directions!' There then followed a two-way torrent of bitter accusations, not the least of which concerned their last night together with the whole party – not one of them younger than sixty. Apparently, they were all gathered in a pub on the front, reliving old memories and indulging in an uproarious rendering of 'We're gonna hang out the washing on the Ziegfried line', when dozens of police cars surrounded the building. 'Come out with your hands up' came the instruction from outside. The entire party was thrown in the cells and not let out till their plane was on the tarmac.

'Good grief!' I was horrified. 'You'll not be going back to *Spain* again, then?'

'Course we will,' said Maggie, 'it was great.'

Ethelbert didn't think so. (I could tell by the way he hobbled off in his half-mast trousers.)

Craig Forester called round at teatime. He seemed really nervous, but as Wilhelmina was upstairs, with Tom, opening their presents, and Maggie was in her bedroom rubbing cream all over Ethelbert's red bits, I did my best to put him at ease straight away. 'It's lovely to see you, Craig,' I said, not forgetting that the last time he was here he'd spent most of the evening snooping. Still, I was hoping he might have come to explain his odd behaviour, and to offer an apology. Of course, I intended to give him every opportunity, because it had been on my mind ever since. And, funnily enough, Craig Forester was growing on me!

When I offered to make him a cup of tea or something, he took my hand as I passed to go into the scullery. 'No, Jessy,' he said, his voice gentle and those navy-blue eyes softly smiling at me. 'Sit down, please. There's something I have to tell you . . . a confession I have to make. And it can't wait.' He looked really serious, and I got the feeling that there was more to it than just taking a sneaky look in a cupboard, or examining the chimney.

'Of course,' I said, sitting down opposite him. 'The tea can wait.'

Unfortunately, it wasn't only the tea that had to wait, because at that moment the horrible Tom came rushing in with the wooden aeroplane Maggie had brought him. 'Look, Mam!' he yelled, diving all over the place as though he were piloting it. 'Look what Maggie got me.' He began blowing raspberries and buzzing the blessed thing in and out of the furniture, missing Craig's nose by a hair's breadth.

Then in came his obnoxious sister, parading a Spanish shawl about her shoulders. 'I shall be a model one day,' she said smugly, 'and travel the world.' (The sooner the better.)

Of a sudden, there came a series of horrifying screams from upstairs. 'Maggie's rubbing cream on Ethelbert's sore arse,' said Tom, quickly perceiving the look on my face and keeping well out of my reach as he continued to dive-bomb all and sundry.

In a minute, Craig was on his feet and making for the front door, 'I'm sorry,' he said with a little smile, 'I'd better go.'

At the door, he kissed me tenderly on the mouth, making me feel warm and comfortable all over. 'What I

141

have to tell you is very important,' he murmured. 'Can I pick you up on Friday? We'll find somewhere quiet where we can talk.'

'I'll look forward to it,' I said, squeezing his hand. I was surprised to find just how *much* I was looking forward to it. But my eager anticipation was somewhat shadowed by the 'very important' thing he had to confess.

Wednesday, February 22nd

There was good news in the post this morning. *I* had two letters, one from Tiffany in Singapore. 'I'm in love,' she wrote. 'I've met an American property developer, and he's going to build me a huge house overlooking Miami Beach.' (All right for some, isn't it, eh?) The other letter was from the Council, saying that their many surveys and meetings had reflected a strong argument for modernizing Casey's Court in preference to demolishing it. (I could have told them that *without* all the blessed squandering of taxpayers' money!) 'However,' they went on to say, 'no final decision has yet been made. The issue will be put forward at the next planners' meeting at the end of the month, when all accrued information will be presented for consideration. Residents of Casey's Court will afterwards be duly notified.'

'I *still* don't trust the buggers,' Sonya declared. ''Appen we oughtta stage a demonstration outside the town hall on the day of the meeting, just to mek certain they do the right thing by us!' Maggie was in full agreement, as were Marny Tupp and the woman from the tripe shop. When I advised caution, however, pointing out that a noisy demonstration might send the whole thing the wrong way,

142

causing certain councillors to vote for demolition, Mrs Arkwright from Rosamund Street was right behind me.

'That's true,' she said knowingly. 'The very same thing happened when folks marched on the town hall to stop Clutters Mill from being pulled down. Oh, that were a grand old building . . . regal and full of memories. Now there's a take-away and a launderette where it used to stand. And one of the very councillors who voted to have it pulled down owns the second-hand car place there. Don't rile them, that's my advice. You've made your protests, you've got your MP fighting on your behalf, you've sent in a strong deputation. So I say leave it be now, and keep your fingers crossed.'

Most folks down Casey's Court thought the same way. 'Let's not rock the boat now,' they told Sonya.

'All right then,' she reluctantly agreed, 'but don't blame me if the buggers *sink* it!' (I do hope she's wrong.)

When Maggie opened *her* letter there were screams and whoops of joy as she grabbed Ethelbert in a sore place. 'What the 'ell's up with yer, woman?' he cried, wincing in pain as she danced him round the room.

'We've got the *key*!' she laughed. 'The key to next door.' Well, there was no stopping her. She rushed out, dragging Ethelbert behind her. 'We shall have to get started on the work,' she bubbled, 'washing, scrubbing . . . papering and shopping. Oh, and we'd best get down to Tipples' yard to see what good stuff he's got. I'm so excited,' she called behind her. 'We'll have a party, Jessy, the noisiest housewarming party Casey's Court's ever seen. We'll get that man from No. 18 to play his band, and oh, Jessy, what a time we'll have!' (There'll be no peace now.)

Later, Maggie asked Sonya to go with them on Saturday to Tipples' yard, because 'you'll be able to knock his prices down better. He'll take more notice of you, being as you've known him a long time.' (It's Maggie's back-handed way of bringing the two of them together, bless her.) At first, Sonya said no. But then, quite unexpectedly, about half an hour later, she said she would. Oh, I do wish they could forget the past and make a future together. I've got a feeling that they were meant for each other.

And another surprising thing that hasn't escaped my notice . . . Sonya seems to have lost her appetite for 'clients' she entertains. 'It must be me age,' she said.

But I told her straight out, 'It's *not* your age. It's your heart . . . you're in love with Tipples, so why don't you admit it?'

She wouldn't, though. 'Yer daft cow!' she said. 'I might 'a known you'd come up wi' some'at bloody sloppy. It's me *age*, I tell yer. Me urges are going.' (They're not. They're just changing direction. And I'm glad.)

Thursday, February 23rd

Barny is deliberately avoiding me. I was fetching the milk in this morning when he got into his car. 'Barny, we need to talk,' I called, beginning to make my way across to him. But he slammed the door shut and accelerated down the road the minute he saw me coming. I don't know what made me do it, but I flung a pint of milk after him. It took me twenty minutes to clear it up, and another ten chasing round the streets after the milkman. 'Well, I'm blowed,' he said, tipping back his cap and looking me up and down with big saucy eyes. 'I've had 'em wink at me through the window and leave me cheeky little notes; I've had 'em very nearly drag me in, the minute the old man's

144

gone to work. But I've *never* had 'em chase after me round the streets in their dressing-gown. Cor, bugger me, darling . . . you *must* be desperate!' (I wouldn't mind, but he's toothless, and ninety if he's a day. Please God I'll never be *that* desperate.)

Poor old Fred Twistle's not mending as fast as they thought. And Bertha's gone from bad to worse. She's rushing about telling all and sundry that he's only brought it on himself, and she doesn't care if he *never* comes home. 'Let him go the way of his precious pigeons,' she said, 'they can all fly off to the happy land together.'

Sonya says she's completely flipped her lid. 'It's *her* they'll be tekking ter the "happy land" afore long,' she warned me, 'an' did yer know that Fung Woo 'ad ter tek 'er 'ome when 'e caught 'er crying all over 'is bean-sprouts?' When I sympathized and said that no, I *didn't* know about that, she shook her strawberry-blonde head and rolled her brown eyes upwards. 'Oh yes,' she said, obviously totally unsympathetic towards any woman who's daft enough to display her weaknesses in public, 'I should steer clear o' that Bertha if I were you. Oh, an' I should steer clear o' beansprouts an' all. They're far too salty as it is.' (Heartless cow!)

That new man in No. 18 told the woman from the tripe shop that he's a retired Salvation Army officer. 'There y'are, Jessy gal,' laughed Sonya, 'I *knew* that feller 'ad been in the army. 'E were probably a squadron-leader or some'at.' Anyway, it seems he's accumulated all those instruments over the years, and he's anxious to get a band started down Casey's Court.

'I doubt whether he'll have much success,' warned the woman from the tripe shop. 'I remember when Paddy Flynn at No. 64 took up the bagpipes. He could never master the blessed things. And it didn't go down too well with the neighbours, I can tell you.'

'Oh?' I said, somewhat bemused. I was still trying to picture this Irishman trying to play the bagpipes.

'Neighbours *hated* it, so they did . . . all that screaming and wailing. It was quite frightful. He gave up the idea after a while, and I can remember the very notice he put up in his window. It said, "Bagpipes for sale (I've tried and tried, but the Lord hasn't answered my prayers)." The man next door put up a notice as well, saying, "Hallelujah! (I've cried and cried and he's answered *mine*.)"'

Sonya's volunteered to play the trombone. 'I allus did like playing wi' things that go in an' out,' she said (you could have fooled me). It seems that half of Casey's Court are queuing up to play in the band. Even little Larkin's been taken on to play the cymbals. 'She'll be as good as a ventriloquist,' said Sonya, 'she'll be able to do it wi'out even *touching* 'em.' Tipples has signed on to play the drums (I think he's done it because he knows Sonya's going to be in the band). Smelly Kelly fancies the trumpet, and the woman from the tripe shop fancies a French horn.

'I allus knew there was more to her than meets the eye,' said Maggie.

Maggie and Ethelbert have opted for the two big oompah things, and *I've* been badgered into playing the other set of drums. I was perfectly honest with the man from No. 18 (a funny little chap, he is, with his stiff little moustache, bald head, and a nose like a lighthouse beacon – Sonya reckons he's a secret boozer). 'You'll have your work cut out, teaching us to play these instruments,' I said, 'even on a crash course. We're all of us tone-deaf, I reckon.'

'Nonsense, woman!' he thundered. 'When *I* say you will play . . . you *will* play!' (I bet Svengali was his dad.)

Friday, February 24th

I got myself all excited about my date with Craig, and then, at ten past two, the headmistress rang up. 'Could you please fetch your Tom from school? He's not at all well, and there are swellings coming up behind his ears. I fear he might be contagious.' (*I* could have told her that.)

'He's got mumps, I'm afraid,' said the doctor, in that peculiarly satisfied way doctors have. 'He is contagious, so keep him in bed, away from your customers, and give him a cuddle now and then.' (Bloody cheek!)

'If *he's* staying at home, so am *I*,' snorted Bossy-boots, ''cause if *he's* convulsive then *I* must be as well. But don't cuddle *me* . . . I'm far too grown up for such things.' (Thank heavens for small mercies.)

Later on, Sonya was 'otherwise engaged' and Maggie was up to her armpits in Ethelbert and distemper. (I could hear the row going at full blast next door. 'Look at my freshly polished windows, you dozy old fool!' yelled Maggie, while Ethelbert was happily slapping the paint on the walls. 'There's great blobs of pink paint splattered all *over* my bloody windows!' Quick as a flash, back came the retort, 'Huh! Well *whose* fault's that then, eh? *Who* chose pink?')

I was desperate for a babysitter, but it seemed that, when their day's work was over, everybody in Casey's Court was off to practise playing their instruments. 'Him at No. 18 intends to have the finest band in the whole of England,' Sonya said proudly. (I wonder if anybody's told Jack Parnell?)

147

There was nothing else for it but to get in touch with Craig and postpone our date. 'I'll come round and stay in the house with you,' he offered. 'I *must* talk to you, Jessy. I have to get something off my chest. It's been worrying me.'

I told him that he couldn't *possibly* come round, Tom being so contagious. We agreed he would collect me Friday next, and I'd be sure to book a babysitter well in advance.

Barny rang. He was really nice. 'I'm sorry, darling,' he said, 'and I hope you understand. But I'm going through a very emotional patch, and I need a month to think our relationship through.' Of course, I reluctantly agreed. But I spent a really miserable evening thinking that he might be about to throw me over for good. (Strange, though, how the thought of Craig gave me a deal of comfort.)

About eleven-thirty, Maggie and Ethelbert staggered in the door, thoroughly exhausted from their efforts with the oompah things. 'Blowing and puffing and dragging it round,' complained Ethelbert, 'I ain't got the strength any more, gal. Honestly, I feel like me light's gawn out.' Just then, there was an electricity cut. When Maggie located the torch and switched it on, we found him bent over the yellow pages, looking under Cake Decorations for Emergency Services.

'You daft old coot,' laughed Maggie, 'where's your glasses?' I wasn't at all surprised when he told her they'd fallen in 'that new dog-loo you med me sink in the yard'. Nor was I surprised when she didn't tell him off. Or he might have reminded her what she said on seeing that loo for the first time. 'You'll *never* train Lucky to sit on *that*,' she said.

It seems that the fellow from No. 18 was so pleased with the practice session that he's called another one on

148

Sunday afternoon. 'The vicar won't take too kindly to that,' I reminded them, 'it is the Sabbath.'

'It won't bother 'im,' said Sonya, ''e's playing your drums while Tom's poorly.' (There's *nobody* craftier than vicars, I don't care what anyone says!)

'Just so long as he knows it's temporary,' I said. (Let him try it on with me and he won't know what's hit him.)

Apparently, the woman from the tripe shop can do things with a French horn that surprised everybody. 'We all know where she gets *that* from, don't we?' Maggie asked Ethelbert.

'Don't look at *me* with yer insinuations, woman,' Ethelbert said in a huff. 'There's no way *I* can be 'er dad . . . the woman's proper ugly!' He was quite put out when Maggie said as far as *she* was concerned that only *strengthened* the case.

Sonya thoroughly enjoyed making noises with the trombone. 'All that pushing and pulling is good fer yer chest,' she smiled. 'The feller from No. 18 said the trombone were *med* fer me. 'E were quite impressed wi' me performance, but 'e said me breathing needed working on. 'E were ever so good, though, 'cause 'e kept an eye on me just ter mek sure me chest were going in an' out at the right time.'

'Kept his eyes *glued* to your chest, don't you mean?' remarked Maggie. 'I'm not surprised Tipples smacked him round the ear with his drumstick. The fellow was blatantly ogling your assets.'

'That Tipples . . . 'e shouldn't jump ter such conclusions,' Sonya replied with a touch of feigned irritation, but she was obviously pleased by Tipples' intervention on her behalf. 'Anybody'd think 'e *owns* me,' she finished with a little smile. On the whole, though, it looks as if we'll have a band, of sorts anyway, to play at the fête.

The trouble is, we'll have to recruit some of the Rosamund Street women to take on the stalls. As Sonya remarked, 'I can't be selling bric-a-brac an' playing a trombone all at the same time.'

Saturday, February 25th

I wish Sonya wouldn't insist on following me into town. I wouldn't mind, but she always manages to show me up one way or another. First of all we had to run like the clappers for the five P.M. bus, then she caught her high heel in a crack, and spent the next hour limping alongside me. Everybody was staring. When we were coming out of Woolworths she went right over on the good heel. It was like something out of a slow-motion film. She lost her balance and staggered forward trying to keep upright. But she'd already gone past the point of no return, so up in the air went her handbag as she landed in a heap at the feet of a bemused road-sweeper. 'Are you all right, luv?' the chubby little fellow asked, bending forward to help her up. Just then, Sonya's handbag came down to earth and caught him a chop in the back of his neck. The poor fellow went cross-eyed as he fell on top of Sonya. *She* quite enjoyed it, but it took a good five minutes for him to recover. In the meantime, somebody stole his trolley. (Is *nothing* sacred?)

Maggie and Ethelbert got some good stuff from Tipples' warehouse (and, according to the tale I got, Tipples and Sonya were getting on like a house on fire). 'He's taking me to the pictures,' Sonya told me afterwards, excited. (She rang me up later, to say he'd actually kissed her. I do hope it's the start of something wonderful.)

Maggie's thrilled to bits with what she got for the

house. There's a sofa with all its stuffing intact, two floral armchairs, and a teak sideboard for the parlour. And, for less than a tenner, she's got a really pretty bedroom suite (I don't think it matters that somebody's scratched 'Kilroy wuz here' on the bed head). Tipples found her a big wooden ottoman containing half a dozen scatter rugs and enough curtaining to go all over the house. 'Go on,' he said, when she gingerly asked the price, 'give us a fiver for the lot.' (Sonya says he's got a heart of gold. She's been singing his praises all day.) Maggie and Ethelbert move in on Monday.

'I reckon they'll end up getting wed,' remarked Maggie. 'They do seem to be head over heels in love.'

Ethelbert told her not to be so easily misled. 'We all thought the same twenty years ago,' he reminded her. 'It went wrong *then*, an' it can go wrong agin.' (I'm on pins, I really am.)

Just as we were about to go to bed there came a frantic knock on the door. 'You two go on up,' I told Maggie and Ethelbert. 'I've got a feeling it might be Barny.' Maggie didn't say anything, but the look she gave me was enough to turn the milk sour.

'Don't yer think it's time yer gave that one 'is marching orders?' asked Ethelbert (looks like Maggie's got him round to her way of thinking). When I told him I was quite old enough to make my own decisions, Maggie collared him by the scruff of his neck and yanked him up the stairs.

'Come on, chichicoo,' she said, 'there's none so blind as them that will not cross the road!' (I'm confused.)

Anyway, it *wasn't* Barny at the door. It was Bertha Twistle. 'Oh, Jessy, Jessy,' she cried, stumbling in and beseeching me with sad tearful eyes, 'what shall I do? Oh, dear God, forgive a foolish old woman . . . whatever shall

I do?' She was in a dreadful state, so I ushered her into the parlour and sat her down, thinking a fresh-brewed cuppa might calm her nerves.

'Now, just you take hold of yourself, Bertha love,' I coaxed. 'I'll get us a drink . . . then you can tell me all about it, eh? Do you take milk and sugar?' She raised her tear-stained face and looked at me as if I was some sort of idiot.

'*Never*,' she said, pulling a face. 'Hot milk and a good helping of brandy, or I'll have nowt at all, thank you very much.' (Silly me.)

When the third brandy had slithered down, Bertha's courage came up. 'I've given all Fred's pigeons away,' she sobbed, holding out her cup for a top-up, 'every last one of 'em. *That's* why I can't face him, don't y'see?' She knocked back the dregs in her cup and thrust it out again. 'And I can't get 'em back, because it were some fellow over Preston way as took 'em.'

'Oh, Bertha, why did you do it? You *know* how fond your Fred is of those pigeons.'

'Oh, I know *that* right enough!' I must have said the wrong thing, because now she was fighting fit. 'Nobody knows better than *me* how much that Pred loves his fidgeons.' When she held out her cup again, I delayed giving her any more brandy. I could tell she'd had more than enough . . . her *nose* would have given the game away, even if she was talking sense. It was mottled red and blue, besides which she'd got her little fat legs all of a tangle when she tried to uncross them.

'Come on, Bertha,' I said, helping her to her feet, 'I'm taking you home. You can tell me all about Fred and his pigeons tomorrow.'

'But *that's* the trouble, Jessy. The poor old sod ain't *got* no pigeons no more, has he, eh? Has he? No, *'course* he

152

hasn't! And *why* not, you may ask; well, because his rotten old woman's given 'em all away.' She was crying again. 'Oh, Jessy, I *do* love the old bugger . . . even if he *does* brefer his pirds to me. I love him, and I want him back aside o' me in our little home, but I'm afeared, because when my Fred finds out what I've done . . . he'll swing for me.'

When her legs buckled under her, I had to prop her up against the wall and fetch Maggie. Ethelbert did offer to help, but Maggie told him to stay where he was and keep the bed warm. 'Save your strength for other things,' she giggled. (I've been labouring under the delusion that life begins at forty. It's obviously *sixty*. Or, in Ethelbert's case, seventy.)

After much grunting, groaning, pushing and pulling, we got Bertha home, where she was given enough black coffee to sink a battleship. Once we were certain that she'd come to no harm, Maggie and I made our way home. 'Thank goodness for that,' I sighed, 'now for a nice warm bed.'

Maggie was first upstairs. 'Now for a nice warm cuddle,' she smiled.

A few minutes later, her voice sailed out of the bed-room. 'Ethelbert Pitts!' she moaned. 'Have you no consideration? You might at *least* have stayed awake!' (I can't help but feel just a *little* bit pleased.)

Sunday, February 26th

Bertha popped round this morning. 'Pinch me, dear,' she said, turning her back and bending over.

'What for?' I asked (well, you would, wouldn't you?).

''Cause I'm not sure whether I'm dead or alive, the way

153

I feel. Oh, but it's my own fault, I'm not denying it.' Straightening up, she turned ever so slowly round, with both hands clasped to her head. 'What's more, Jessy dear, I don't deserve friends like you and Maggie. I've been an absolute prig.' She went on to explain how she hadn't known which way to turn when her Fred was taken ill. She loved him so much. 'Well, we've been together a long time, me and my old feller. And I was that hurt when he showed them bloody pigeons more affection than *ever* he's shown me. Do you know, Jessy . . . the very first thing the old fool asked after when he regained consciousness was them blessed pigeons?' She did look devastated, the poor soul, even when I explained how some folk find it very difficult to demonstrate their love for somebody else. 'I know that now, lass. When I stopped to think, I realized that *I* had never told *him* just how much he means to me, and no doubt he thinks I care more for my cats than I do for him.'

There was nobody more relieved than I was to hear Bertha Twistle say that, bless her old heart. What's more, she's found a way to make amends. As I told Maggie, 'She's going to the infirmary to arrange for his homecoming, and she's going to confess everything. But it'll be all right, because she's made a deal with some fellow to buy a consignment of baby pigeons from a particular racing strain. And she reckons Fred will forgive her, because he's always wanted a batch of pigeons from that strain . . . it seems they're very highly sought after and valuable.'

Maggie wasn't impressed. 'Valuable racing strain indeed! Huh! If I know that daft Bertha, she'll end up buying a batch of pullets.' (Oh, ye of little faith, I thought. Then I thought, she wouldn't would she? No, of *course* she wouldn't.) All the same, I asked Ethelbert.

154

'Bugger me,' he said, 'Bertha lived with pigeons long enough to know one from a *pullet*.' Honestly, that Maggie had me worried for a minute.

Tom's been a real little misery all day, whine whine whine. 'He's getting on my nerves, Mam,' Wilhelmina complained, 'can't you shut him up?' Then she threw her jigsaw at him. 'It's not fair,' she said, storming off in a temper, 'nobody asked *me* whether I wanted a rotten brother!' (Nobody asked *me* whether I wanted two rotten kids either!)

Granny Grabber's chimney caught alight and the fire brigade was called. It seemed she had one of her fits and was chasing her little dog, Skidaddle, all over the place when the draught flamed the fire. The woman from the tripe shop told Sonya later, 'I were just 'aving me tea when it started . . . all this frightful hollering and squealing.'

'Good Lord,' exclaimed Sonya, enjoying every minute, 'poor Granny Grabber. I expect the old dear was terrified.'

'No, no, you silly woman,' retorted the woman from the tripe shop, ''tweren't *Granny Grabber* who was screaming and hollering. It was the poor bloody dog. Oh, dear me, you shoulda seen it tear up the road when the fireman let it out. Its little ears were flat back and its eyes were big wi' fright. Oh, and its poor little arse looked just like one o' them monkeys you see in the zoo . . . all red an' bald it were.' (It wouldn't surprise me if we never saw Skidaddle again, red, bald, or otherwise.)

It's been one of those days when you wonder how you find the strength to go on. I've lost count of how many times Maggie came rushing in to drag me off so I could give her my opinion on the colour of her curtains, or whether the lamp-shades match the distemper, or did I think the sideboard was in the right place, and should she put the oblong mat or the half-moon in front of the fireplace? Oh, and was it right that, if the feet of your bed faced the window, it was a sure sign that the bogey-man was coming for you? 'Only I wouldn't want that to happen, Jessy,' she said, 'me and Ethelbert aren't ready to go yet, on account of we're just starting out on the highway of wedded bliss, and we're too much in love to have it all spoiled now. Besides,' she added with a twinkle in her eye, 'there's things we haven't done yet, and oh, Jessy . . . there are so many adventures awaiting us.'

I put her mind at rest straight away. 'Take no notice of those old superstitions,' I told her. 'You face the foot of your bed to the window if you want to. If the bogey-man's coming for anybody, it'll be for *me*, and, the way *I* feel, it should come as no surprise.' (I need a holiday.)

Barny waved at me today, but I wish he hadn't because now I can't get him out of my mind. Craig rang and told me not to forget our date on Friday. How could I? I'm itching to know what it is he's going to 'confess'. I expect it's something soppy. Perhaps he's going to say he can't live without me. (I get these fanciful ideas sometimes. Usually when I'm feeling suicidal.)

The band seems to be coming along a treat. That man from No. 18 can certainly get the best out of people. 'Me and Ethelbert didn't know one end of an oompah from the other,' bragged Maggie. 'Now it's just Ethelbert who's confused.' (What's new?) Apparently Tipples has a natural bent towards playing the drums, while Marny Tupp found *he* has a natural bent towards other things (Sonya to be precise). When he got a bit too close for comfort, Tipples lobbed him one. They've both been banned from the next practice session. 'Ooh, yer shoulda seen my Tipples,' (*my* Tipples indeed!). 'Came rushing ter me rescue, 'e did. Oh, 'e's a right little tiger an' no mistake.' (I'm so pleased.)

Maggie didn't move into her house today after all. Ethelbert put his foot through the lavatory pan, so they've to wait for the Council to come and fit another. 'Whatever was he doing with his foot near the lavatory pan?' I wanted to know.

'Ask no questions, get told no lies,' Maggie retorted. (Now my imagination's running riot.)

Tuesday, February 28th

I had a letter from Tiffany. 'I'm worn out,' she wrote. 'Honestly, he's so virile, I don't get any rest at all.' (I hope she doesn't expect *me* to sympathize.)

On the other hand, Sonya seems to be running down her list of 'clients'. When I mentioned it, she went all shy. 'Tipples takes up more of my time these days,' she said. Then she called me a silly cow when I warned her not to get her hopes up, because it all went wrong before. Learn to crawl before you run, my mother always used to say. (Or it could be that I'm jealous.)

I've got a feeling that Sonya's keeping something from me. I do hope she's not pregnant.

Wednesday, March 1st

There are days when I feel all alone in the world.

Thursday, March 2nd

The Council men came to fit Maggie's new lavatory. 'Goodness, that was quick,' she remarked.

'Aye. The guv said we'd best get it done, else you'll be chaining yourself to our compound gates,' came the blunt reply. (Her reputation goes before her.)

Tom's back at school, and here's a funny thing. I actually *missed* him. 'Fancy that,' I told Sonya.

"Tain't that surprising,' she said. 'Kids 'ave a way o' creeping under yer skin.' (Like the plague.)

Friday, March 3rd

It rained relentlessly all day.

A beautiful bouquet of flowers arrived this morning. 'Gawd luv us,' exclaimed Sonya, 'them's grand. Who sent 'em?' As there was no card, I couldn't tell her. However, some fifteen minutes later, I saw Barny getting into his car and, just before he pulled away, he turned, smiled and gave me the friendliest wave. Sonya thought Craig sent the flowers. I was sure it must be Barny.

At eight-thirty, I was dressed in my best blue frock, with a Marks & Sparks shawl draped over my shoulders and my face made up to hide any bags or worry-lines. 'You'll do,' Maggie said, 'but you're no film star.' (Who needs friends?)

However, from the moment he arrived, Craig made me

158

feel like a million dollars. He looked quite handsome, I thought, in a dark blazer, with grey trousers and a black polo-neck shirt. It *was* him who had sent the flowers. 'They're lovely,' I told him, sipping my wine over the candlelit table.

'Not as lovely as *you*,' he said, his deep-blue eyes smiling into mine.

All evening, there was no mention of the 'urgent' thing he had to confess. But after he'd brought me home, and we were sitting in the van watching the rain, out it all tumbled. And my goodness, what a revelation it was. It turns out that old Pops, who left me the barber-shop, was quite a Jack-the-lad in his day. Apparently, and in spite of all his philandering, there was only ever *one* child, and this by a woman who kept house for him at one time. Her name was Peggy, and she gave old Pops a son. Old Pops, however, was not cut out to be either a dad or a husband. Consequently, he turfed Peggy and the child out of his house. That child was Craig.

'I grew up not knowing who my father was,' he said, 'until a few months ago, when I lost my mother. When she knew how ill she was, she told me everything.' For a while, Craig sat quiet in the car, seeming so lost in painful memories that he couldn't bring himself to say any more.

Feeling deeply moved, I reached out to touch his hand, thinking how fond I had become of this gentle, warm-hearted man, who was so different from the arrogant, self-centred Barny. 'It's all right, Craig,' I murmured, leaning over to place a soft consoling kiss on his face, 'I understand how upset you must have been.'

Of a sudden, he was talking again, this time in an angry voice and thumping his clenched fist against the steering-wheel. 'Upset!' He began to laugh softly. 'I wasn't *upset*, Jessy . . . I was bloody furious! I came to Casey's Court with murder in my heart. Then when I found that this "father" of mine was gone, and you were the owner of his property, I'll be honest, Jessy, I wanted to throw you out and claim what I thought was rightfully mine. I couldn't see beyond all the anger and resentment which I'd been bottling up since losing my mother.' He turned and smiled sadly and I felt my heart going out to him. 'She was a good woman, Jessy. Loving and loyal, and in all the hard times when she was raising me, not *once* did she come to him for help.' He was looking at me in a way that reached right into my soul. '*You* remind me of her, Jessy. You have that same gentle quality about you, and you care for others, I know that. You have the same kind of beauty too . . . oh, I don't mean you have the sort of looks that would knock a fellow off his feet, because there's nothing striking about you . . . except maybe your pretty smiling eyes,' (I felt a bit deflated) 'but you have a special beauty that shines out from *inside*.' After that, I was putty in his hands. When he tenderly drew me towards him, I was actually longing for him to kiss me. Then, when he brought his mouth down on mine, I was not surprised that I didn't hear bells ringing, or that my heart wasn't palpitating the way it did when Barny kissed me. Nor was I surprised at that warm pleasant feeling which spread over me as it always did when Craig touched me. But, unlike before, there was a strange emotion taking hold of me, and a reluctance to let go of him.

When, after a while, he eased me away, I found that I was actually trembling. 'Jessy,' he said, 'I think I've loved you from the first moment I saw you.' All in a minute, I felt worried, insecure, and the only thing I could think about was Barny. 'All right,' Craig said, obviously sensing my dilemma, 'I know you're spoken for, and maybe I've done wrong in telling you how I feel.'

'No, no, it's all right. It's *me* . . . I'm just not sure, that's all.' I liked him a lot. But did I *love* him? I had to be certain.

Now he was telling me how his mother described her life with old Pops. 'She did love him, you know. And he had a fair bit of money, what with the shop, and running an illegal bookie's on the side . . . well, he had quite a bit put by.'

I'd heard how old Pops was never what he seemed. 'What is it you're trying to tell me, Craig?' I asked, because I could sense there was something behind all this.

'My mother told me how the old bugger used to stuff wads of notes into a battered old tin and, when he thought nobody was looking, hide it . . . up the chimney, under the floorboards, anywhere he thought it couldn't be seen.'

Everything was becoming clear. 'You! It was *you* who took up the floorboards in my parlour. *You* who badgered me time and time again to sell my home.' Now it was *my* turn to be furious. The fellow was nothing but a snoop and an opportunist. He was trying to manipulate me in the very same way that Barny had. But no. Barny *wasn't* as bad after all. It *hadn't* been him who'd been harassing me over the shop. It was Craig Forester. Oh, what an *idiot* I'd been. No wonder Barny needed time to think over whether he really wanted to marry me. No wonder! I had completely and cruelly misjudged him. 'Don't you *ever* set foot in my shop again!' I told Craig Forester. 'I want nothing more to do with you.' Then, ignoring his protests that I had it all wrong, that not only did he love me but he wanted to *marry* me, I scrambled out of the van. 'Get out of Casey's Court!' I screamed, standing up to my ankles in a puddle of water. 'I was a fool to let you take advantage of me.' I was not unaware that curtains were shifting all along the street, nor that Maggie had her

161

face glued to the window. There came a familiar raucous laugh and a shout of 'Go to it, Jessy gal. Sounds like yer 'ad a good time!' I quickly fled into the house, bolting the door after me.

'Oh, Maggie, what is it about me that brings out the worst in men?' I wondered.

'I have no idea, young lady,' she replied, ushering Ethelbert out the back door. 'I'm just the same, though. I expect it's a gift.'

Saturday, March 4th

I'm quite surprised that there's been no word from Craig. I fully expected him to be knocking on the door, or sheepishly creeping into the salon, but I realize now that he's not the sort to do that. Every time the phone rang, I was sure it would be him. 'You tell the snake in the grass I want nothing more to do with him,' I instructed Sonya, when she answered the calls. But they were never him. Nor did he call round, and there were no flowers bedecked with cards of apology.

'Yer *want* 'im ter gerrin touch, don't yer, gal? Admit it,' teased Sonya. I left her in no doubt whatsoever that I never wanted to set eyes on Craig Forester again. (Funny thing is, I'm not sure about my own feelings.)

'Strange business, though, ain't it, Jessy?' she remarked, after I'd told her what happened. 'I find it 'ard ter believe it were Craig Forester who tore up the floorboards, and badgered yer ter sell the shop an' everything.'

'Oh, it *was* him right enough,' I assured her, 'he as much as admitted it.'

'But all this business about hoards o' money an' that. I

162

don't know as I believe it, gal. If yer recall, some time back when yer couldn't get the fire going . . . didn't yer find an old tin stuffed up the chimney?' (Oh, yes. I'd quite forgotten that.) 'Well, there weren't no treasure in there. Unless yer count that correspondence from Maggie Thatcher as treasure. No, gal . . . I reckon Craig's mam must 'ave imagined it, or old Pops spent the bloody lot afore 'e died.' She gave out a great roar of appreciation. 'An' who can blame the poor bugger, eh? 'E never went anywhere in 'is latter years, and . . .' Of a sudden, she grabbed me by the arm. 'Hey! That's *right*, Jessy gal. Old Pops never went anywhere, an' 'e never spent a penny when an 'alfpenny would do.'

I saw what she was getting at. 'There's *another* alternative,' I said, getting caught up in her excitement. 'Suppose . . . just *suppose* that there was a *second* box, where he kept his more valuable bits and pieces?'

Once the possibility had presented itself, it wouldn't go away. Maggie and Ethelbert were all for tearing the house apart bit by bit. 'I tell yer what, Jessy,' Ethelbert said, jumping up and down with excitement (Maggie warned him to calm down. She didn't want *him* wetting his pants). 'That Craig Forester is probably right. What's more, I knew his mam, Peggy. She were a grand little soul and didn't deserve what the old bugger did. The whole o' Casey's Court were up in arms when 'e threw 'er out. What's more, little Peggy were no liar. If she told Craig there were a box stuffed with wads o' notes, then there *must* be such a box!'

There was nothing else for it now but to do two things straight away. One was to contact Craig at the lodgings he had told me about. The other was to turn the house and salon upside down till we found old Pops's 'treasure'. 'And *if* we find it,' I told one and all, 'it belongs to his son, Craig.' I was adamant on that. And everybody was in full agreement. So it was arranged that we should all meet in the parlour after dinner, and we'd all take one section of the house each. 'Cor!' exclaimed Tom. 'We can all pretend to be pirates, searching for Captain Hook's gold.' Wilhelmina promptly instructed him to grow up. Then she went off to make them a paper eye-patch each.

I tried all afternoon to get in touch with Craig. I really felt that I'd done him an injustice.

'I'm sorry, luv,' his landlady finally informed me, 'he's gone.'

'Gone?' My heart sank like a weight inside me. 'Gone *where*? Will he be back?'

'I'm afraid not, dearie. Leastwise, perhaps not till weekend. He's supposed to be coming back to fetch the last of his things when he's found new lodgings down south.' Apparently there was no way she could contact him. But yes, she would give him my message when he returned at the weekend. 'That is, *if* he returns. I have a feeling he might not.'

'Please,' I begged, 'if he *does*, tell him that Jessica rang, and that I'm sorry about the things I said. And, please, make sure you let him know to contact me straight away. I believe him. Just tell him that . . . I *believe* him.' I had a horrible feeling I might never see him again.

By midnight, we were all shattered. Sonya fetched Tipples round. ''E's got big muscles,' she said proudly. 'If there's owt 'ere, my Tipples'll soon find it.' But, in spite of taking up the floor bit by bit and examining the cavity beneath, we found nothing there (except a dead rat and a pair of lacy bras). We searched every possible nook, cranny and crack. We shifted all the furniture in every room, and we even took the lavvy apart. Until, in the

164

end, we had to admit that old Pops didn't have a secret hoard of money after all.

'It's no good, Jessy,' Tipples had worked harder than any of us, 'there's no place else ter look, so we might as well call it a day.' The decision was unanimous.

'I expect the old sod left instructions fer the undertaker ter bury it wi' 'im,' Sonya said. Well, at least we tried, and did everything humanly possible, I thought. But, it didn't console me, and I found myself thinking more and more about Craig Forester.

Ah well, goodnight, Lord. It's two o'clock of a morning and I'm tired. I thought you said somewhere, 'Seek, and ye shall find.' (It seems we can't even rely on *you*, eh?)

Hold on! There's Maggie and Ethelbert outside under the window, shouting and hollering. I suppose I'd best see what they want.

3 A.M.

Eureka!!!

We found it! We found old Pops's tin . . . crammed tight with wads of tenners, twenties and fifties, just like Craig's mam said.

It was Ethelbert's brainwave that did the trick. Apparently, he woke Maggie up, all of a dither. 'I've got it, gal,' he shouted, frightening the life out of her. (I bet she wondered what he meant!) It seems old Pops had a saying, and Ethelbert had suddenly remembered it. 'There were some'at bothering me when I fell asleep,' he explained, 'an' I couldn't quite put me finger on it.' (I *am* surprised. Maggie must be slipping.) 'Anyway, old Pops allus used ter wink an' tell folks that "where there's muck, there's brass". It were *that* as got me thinking. *Where* d'yer find

165

muck, eh? Why . . . in a *dustbin*.' And, bless his old cotton socks, he was right. Well, almost, but it pointed us in the right direction. The tin was buried under the slab where the dustbin stands.

'The crafty ol' bugger,' laughed Ethelbert, prising open the lid, to find it packed solid with all those big value notes. Altogether, there was over six thousand pounds, two gold signet rings and the deeds to a chalet at Scarborough. 'D'yer know, gal,' declared Ethelbert, 'I remember the *very* card game when 'e won that chalet. An' ter this very day, I were sure ol' Pops 'ad long since sold it.' (Hmh! What care I for Tiffany's house overlooking Miami Beach? It can't hold a candle to a chalet in Scarborough.)

Sunday, March 5th

I rang Craig's landlady again. 'No. I told you, dearie . . . if he *does* make his way back, it won't be till next weekend. I'll pass on your message, don't worry.' But I *do* worry, because he might never come back, and then he won't get what's rightfully his.

'Tell the truth, Jessy.' Sonya's convinced I love him. 'It ain't the *money* yer want 'im ter come back for, is it, eh? You want 'im ter come back fer *you*, don't yer?' (I wish I knew. But then there's Barny.)

'Forget that one,' urged Sonya, 'there's nowt but 'eartache there, gal.'

'Why do you go on and on about him? It only makes it that much harder for me,' I told her.

'There's only one way ter settle this, me darling,' she said, 'an' mebbe we can get ter the bottom of it once an' fer all . . . 'cause, though I've got me suspicions, I ain't got no real proof.'

166

'Proof of *what*?' I wanted to know. 'Look, Sonya, I'm well aware that he's been two-timing me, but we're trying to work that out. He's taking time out to rethink our relationship, and, in view of the fact that I wrongly accused him of trying to buy me out, I think I owe him the time he needs. Besides, I can forgive him his one indiscretion.'

'Happen yer can. But I wonder if yer could forgive 'im *more* than one? And, more important, gal . . . could yer *live* wi' it?'

'Oh, come on, Sonya. You're not trying to tell me he's playing around with *other* women?' The thought was too much.

'Look 'ere, Jessy. If yer think that dark buxom beauty were just a passing fancy, then yer in fer a very big disappointment. I've a feeling that 'e's more besotted than yer think. An' worse still, gal, if my instincts are right, an' they usually are, I don't think 'e'll *ever* bc able ter give 'er up . . . not even if you an' 'im got wed.'

I refused to listen to any more. '*Prove* it,' I challenged. She told me she'd be round tomorrow evening, when we'd settle it one way or the other. (All this aggravation, and I've run out of cod liver oil.)

Monday, March 6th

After a deal of argument, when I made it quite clear to Sonya that it was a bit much to go knocking on Barny's door at half-past nine at night, she finally persuaded me that it was absolutely essential for my own peace of mind. 'Yer my best pal, Jessy,' she said. 'An' I'm not gonna stand by while 'e does the dirty on yer. There's just *one* question I want ter ask 'im. Then we'll see. We'll see.'

Well, we *saw* right enough! And *what* we saw was a sight I'll never forget. As we approached Barny's house, we could hear the music belting from his front parlour. A gyrating figure was casting shadows on the curtains, which were drawn, and my first thought was that he'd got 'her' in there again. 'I don't want to talk to him,' I told Sonya, my legs all a-tremble. But she grabbed hold of my arm and propelled me forward.

'It's now or never,' she declared, and I got the feeling I was being led into something terrible.

We knocked on the door, but the music was so loud he obviously couldn't hear us. 'Round the back,' Sonya decided, pulling me with her. Once there, she knocked even more loudly. Nothing. Then she pushed against the door and it swung open.

'I'm not going in there uninvited.' I was shocked that she should even think such a thing.

'Yer bloody well are!' Tightening her grip on my arm, she crept forward in the dark.

'Barny,' I yelled, hoping we'd be saved at the last, 'yoo, hoo, Barny, are you there?'

'Course 'e's there, yer daft bugger!' Sonya has an effective way of shutting you up. So we went along the passage, towards the shaft of light beneath the parlour door. (My stomach was turning somersaults, and I've never felt so sick in all my life.)

Once there, with me protesting all the way, but held secure in Sonya's vice-like grip, Sonya gently inched the door open. And there was a long-legged figure, clad only in fine black-seamed tights, red high-heeled shoes, and a scarlet French camisole. The perfume wafted into my nostrils. She was moving in rhythm to the music, totally oblivious of our presence, and looking more glamorously seductive than I could ever achieve in a million years. I

168

knew then that there was no way I could compete with such magnificence. 'I've seen enough,' I murmured to Sonya, wanting to get away quickly, before Barny returned . . . no doubt stripped naked and carrying two martinis. But, even as I spoke, my eyes were fascinated by the woman's movements, and I couldn't take my eyes off her. It wasn't just her lovely underclothes, nor those long shapely legs that held me spellbound. There was something else. Something . . . not quite right.

Of a sudden, Sonya stepped forward and flicked the record-player off. The silence was deafening, as the buxom beauty swung round to stare at us in horror. For a minute I was struck speechless; then, like a thunderbolt, it hit me. 'Barny!' It was Barny! I stood there with my mouth open. I couldn't believe what was in front of my eyes.

'Forgot ter put yer wig on, did yer, sweetie?' asked Sonya. And I turned to run away as fast as my legs would take me. Barny! I still can't believe it. But I saw it. I actually *saw* it with my own eyes.

There's Sonya now, on the pavement outside and yelling up at my bedroom. 'I tried ter tell yer, gal, but I knew yer wouldn't be able ter 'andle it. Now *me*, well . . . I can tek it all in my stride, 'cause I've 'ad the experience, don't yer see? I remember one feller thought 'e were an *elephant* . . . used ter swing 'is trunk about an' nibble doughnuts wi' it.' (I know she means well, bless her, but somehow it doesn't help.)

Tuesday, March 7th

I had a terrible night; kept dreaming about elephants dressed in French camisoles.

This morning I found a note pushed through the letter box. It was from Barny, and it read:

Dear Jessy, I know you must have been shocked by what you saw, and I'm sorry. You can understand now my dilemma about you and me getting married. There is no way I could commit myself to being a husband and raising a family. I love myself the way I am.

Goodbye,
Barny.

'The bugger's gone,' Sonya told me later. 'Snuck off, bag an' baggage, like a thief in the night. An' good shuts, that's what I say.' (Come to think of it, so do I.) All the same, I can't help but feel sad about the whole thing, so I've banned the subject of Barny Singleton from these premises.

Wednesday, March 8th

Everything's happening at once. Sonya came in this morning, grinning from ear to ear. 'I didn't want to tell yer afore, Jessy gal,' she said, all shy and silly, 'but I've got some *wonderful* news . . . if yer ain't guessed already?'

'You're not . . . pregnant?'

'Naw, I'm not *that* stupid, gal.'

'What, then?'

'Me an' Tipples. After all these years, 'e's finally gonna mek an honest woman o' me.' Oh, I was really chuffed about it, although I chided her for not telling me earlier, because it seems that not only have the banns been read and everything, but the happy day is on *Saturday*!

'Good grief!' It was something of a shock. 'There's your reception to be planned. Maggie will insist on baking the cake, and oh, Wilhelmina will want to be bridesmaid.' In a minute, we were cuddling each other and laughing.

'Whatever would I do wi'out yer, Jessy darling?' she roared. From then on, the arrangements were to take priority over everything else.

'I'm sure Craig wouldn't mind you taking your honeymoon in that chalet at Scarborough.' I felt instinctively that he wouldn't mind one little bit. (But, oh, wouldn't it be nice if he was here for me to ask?)

'Ye'll be me Maid of Honour, won't you?' asked Sonya. Of course I said I would, although I was beginning to feel more like an *old* maid!

Thursday, March 9th

I've been in bed all day. I think it's the shock coming out. Maggie says it's constipation. Tom says I'm pretending ''cause you only want to be fussed'. (So what!)

Friday, March 10th

This morning, I got just the thing to put me on top of the world. It was a letter from the Council. Everybody in Casey's Court has been informed that the houses will *not* be demolished! Instead, they're all to be extensively modernized.

Within two minutes of the postman leaving, everybody

was out on the street, whooping and hollering. Marny Tupp even hung out his Union Jack, and the woman from the tripe shop went running up and down the street, yelling, 'Come and get your free black puddings.'

'Not bloody likely,' roared Sonya. 'Them's the same ones yer were selling *last* year!' Everybody laughed, and began gathering in little groups. Of a sudden, somebody shouted, 'Let's have a street party!' The cry was taken up, and one thing led to another. By half-past ten, it had been decided. There was going to be a street party the like of which hadn't been seen since Queen Elizabeth's Coronation. Even the man from No. 18 got carried away. 'We'll have the band playing,' he said. 'They'll be ready.' (Not from what *I've* heard.)

Maggie was thrilled to bits. 'We'll make it my house-warming party as well,' she shouted. 'It's open house for one and all.' Then I gave out the exciting news about it being Tipples and Sonya's wedding-day. That did it.

'Yer daft bugger,' said Sonya, grinning from ear to ear, 'there'll be no 'olding 'em now!' (I don't care!)

Saturday, March 11th

This day will go down in my calendar as the best day of my life.

All morning, folk were rushing about; men putting out the tables and hanging the tattered remains of the very same bunting that decorated the streets on VE day. The women spent hours baking and the band started practising at eight-thirty A.M. (The noise was frightening.)

At two o'clock we all made our way down to pack the church till it was bursting at the seams. I felt so proud

172

when Tipples put the ring on Sonya's finger and the vicar pronounced them man and wife.

Afterwards we all made our way back to begin the celebrations. The vicar came too. I got a lift with Sonya and Tipples on his rag-a-bone cart.

It was great! There were the newly-weds, dancing on the cobbles to the music of the band, the folk all laughing and having a wonderful time. Then, about five o'clock, I saw Craig Forester's old van come creeping into Casey's Court. My heart soared, and when he came to stand beside me I felt like a silly schoolgirl. 'Are we friends, then?' he asked. My answer was to fling my arms round his neck.

'We've found your treasure,' I told him.

'Oh? But I've got the only treasure I want, right here,' he said. Then he took me in his arms and kissed me. (I think it's true love after all.)

Later, Wilhelmina came running out of the house. 'Tiffany called,' she shouted above the street noise. 'She says to tell you he's done the dirty on her. He's run off with a brassy tart, and she's heartbroken.' (So it's good-bye Miami Beach.)

Of a sudden, they were hoisting Tipples and Sonya on to the rag-a-bone cart, which had been decorated from top to bottom with paper flowers and coloured ribbons – even the old horse had a chrysanthemum in her ear. 'Go on!' somebody yelled, smacking the horse's rump. 'Off you go and enjoy yourselves.'

I cried my eyes out when I looked up to see Tipples and Sonya standing atop the waggon. Tipples was holding the reins and looking swell in his new suit and flat cap. Sonya had on a bright red two-piece and a big-brimmed black hat with a blue paper rose on it. 'You look after my pal Jessy,' she called to Craig Forester.

'You can be sure of it,' he shouted back.

Then somebody thrust glasses in our hands, topped them up with fizzy wine, and everybody raised their drinks to the rag-a-bone cart. 'Bottoms up, me darlings,' the toast was called.

'Bottoms up!' came the cry from every direction. And, as the cart disappeared round the corner, I started crying again – until Craig caught me in his arms. 'I love you, Jessica Jolly,' he said.

'And I love you,' I told him, feeling that, at long last, things were going to be all right.

Fred Twistle was fetched home this afternoon, and Bertha must have shown him the 'baby pigeons' she'd bought for him, because everybody collapsed in fits of laughter when his voice came sailing through the air.

'Yer daft sod! Them's not pigeons! They're bloody cockatiels!'

Here we go again. There's no peace down Casey's Court.